W. J. Corbett
Dear Grumble

Illustrated by Tony Ross

MAMMOTH

First published in Great Britain 1989
by Methuen Children's Books Ltd
Published 1991 by Mammoth
an imprint of Reed Consumer Books Ltd
Michelin House, 81 Fulham Road, London SW3 6RB
and Auckland, Melbourne, Singapore and Toronto

Reprinted 1992

Text copyright © W. J. Corbett 1989
Illustrations copyright © Tony Ross 1989

ISBN 0 7497 0114 5

A CIP catalogue record for this title
is available from the British Library

Printed in Great Britain
by Cox & Wyman Ltd, Reading, Berkshire

Contents

They Came for a Goldfish

Tom and Clare Price sat on their front garden gate with a bag of old woollens at their feet. Each day their friends had called with a bouncing ball, hoping to tempt them to a game in the park. But the Prices refused to be lured from their perch. They had more important fish to fry, or rather cherish. They were waiting patiently to hear the sound of hooves clip-clopping up the lane, longing to hear the squeal of iron-shod wheels on tarmac and the familiar cry of 'any old rags'. From Monday to Friday they had been waiting – surely the rag-and-bone man would call today. . . .?

Inside their house everything was ready. The bowl their father had found in the attic had been dusted and now sat sparkling on the dining-room

7

table. Just like a real pond it had a layer of sand and gravel on the bottom, also a large knobbly rock for things to hide behind. To make it even more home-like Tom and Clare had popped in a concrete snail and a plastic frond of weed their father had bought them from the Greenway Pet Centre on his way home from the office, even though he hated shopping at any of the Greenway shops. The bowl was now filled with clear tap water and all-in-all the effect was beautiful. The children felt that it was a home any swimmer would be proud to live in. Especially in the light from the reading lamp they had pinched from their father's 'do not disturb' room. The only thing missing was a goldfish to try it out.

It was midday. Clare was just about to nip indoors for two marmite sandwiches and two glasses of orange when they heard the sound of a horse and cart coming up the lane. Whooping with relief they raced down the lane to meet it, Tom struggling to balance the awkward weight of the plastic bag slung over his slight shoulders. But the excitement of their dash down the lane was nothing compared with the astonishing sight that met their eyes as the horse and cart came round the bend in the lane. They stared in amazement. The rag-and-bone man reined in his tired old horse, his false teeth slipping sideways as he grinned down at them. He knew perfectly well what the children were goggling at but

8

being a bit of a tease, he pretended not to notice. He behaved so matter-of-factly that Tom and Clare began to believe they were seeing things. But they weren't.

The bend in the lane was beginning to cram up with nearly every child in the village. The news had spread like wild-fire and they'd tied their protesting dogs to the bench legs in the park to hare down for the bend in the lane. They could hardly contain themselves. There wasn't a child who wouldn't have given his right arm for a bag of old woollens. But being practical and loyal they were ready to back the dark-haired Prices in the price war they knew was soon to begin. Soon their advice was drowning out the old man's wheedling tone as he pushed his cap to the back of his head and began to speak.

'Will you lot shut up?' snapped Tom. 'Clare and me are trying to hear what the rag-and-bone man is saying.'

'Tell the old man to stop whispering then,' shouted a little pony-tailed girl from the back of the crush. 'And you can warn him that we aren't interested in balloons on sticks. Tell him we are more interested in what he's got tied to the back of his cart.'

'Mind your own business, Felicity Greenway,' said Clare, sharply. 'Where's *your* bag of old woollens?'

Felicity Greenway was always poking her

posh nose in things that didn't concern her. To shut her up the Price supporters pulled her blonde pony-tail and stamped on the toes of her brand-new trainers. But, even so, it was hard to remain quiet when they themselves were so desperate to ask the rag-and-bone man about the amazing object tied to the back of his cart by a tatty piece of string. They were also agog to

learn just how many old woollens such a desirable property was worth. They stopped talking, for they realised they were present at the most historic bit of dickering in the history of the world.

'Shall I start my sales pitch again, then?' asked the rag-and-bone man, his false teeth almost popping out of his mouth as he grinned even

wider at Tom and Clare. He ignored the groans from the audience and began. 'Right, for a small bag of old woollens I can offer a balloon on a stick . . .'

'We've already said we don't want balloons,' yelled Felicity, tugging her pony-tail free from the grasp of a scowling boy and pushing her way to the front of the crowd. 'We have all the balloons we need in this village, thank you very much. Make us another offer, rag-and-bone man.'

'We won't tell you again, Greenway,' warned Tom, angrily prizing her fingers from his arm. Felicity was always trying to touch him and make more of their cool relationship. 'Clare has already told you to keep your sharp nose out of other people's affairs.'

Clare spoke to the grinning old man. 'We appreciate your kind balloon offer, but Tom and me still have some left from last Christmas. Perhaps you have some other things we could look at? Something a little larger, perhaps?'

The village children groaned again as they gazed raptly up at the 'something a little larger'. But having no old woollens themselves they could only pray that Tom and Clare would make the right choice, and never in a million years, settle for less than what they had all set their hearts on.

'Okay, let me see now,' teased the rag-and-bone man. He twisted in his seat and surveyed his rag-piled, balloon-decked cart. 'How about a goldfish? For a large bag of best-quality old woollens, two, even.'

'Keep your goldfish,' cried a frustrated Felicity, rudely. 'We all have large aquariums stuffed full of coloured fish in this village. Why don't you state your terms for the "something a little larger" we have all set our hearts on?'

'Because your heart doesn't come into it,' fumed Tom, shrugging her sneaking arm from around his waist. 'As we Prices are the only ones with old woollens, the man is only concerned with our hearts.'

'Even though our hearts are not a bit set on a goldfish, two, even,' said a firm Clare, looking the old man straight in his twinkling eye. She lied, 'Actually, we Prices have never been gold-fish people. They are so boring. So what else have you got on your cart? Something tied to the back of it, perhaps?'

'Are you Prices blind or daft?' yelled Felicity, her blonde hair wild and matted from all the vicious tugging, her toes throbbing from all the cruel stamping. But for once she didn't care about looking perfect. Her voice rose to a scream as she pointed. 'Any fool can see what the rag-and-bone man has got tied to the back of his cart.'

She began to dash around shaking her head in

disbelief. She didn't realise that Tom and Clare and every village child knew perfectly well what was tied to the back of the old man's rickety cart. She couldn't understand that the Prices were pretending to be casual to get the best possible deal for it because the rag-and-bone man was notorious for demanding more old woollens when customers seemed over eager. As if noticing it for the first time, the old man glanced at the back of his cart.

'Well, if I can't interest you in balloons or goldfish, two, even, all I've got left is my Special Offer. You've noticed him, I suppose?'

The children groaned. Felicity seemed about to have a fit.

'Actually, we have noticed him,' Clare admitted, trying to sound casual. 'Only out of the corner of our eyes, of course.'

'Of course,' replied the old man with another slip-tooth grin. But his eyes were suddenly shrewd. 'He's a cracker, don't you think? So, we're interested, are we?'

'He does look quite nice,' said Tom as coolly as he could. He wrenched his hypnotised gaze from the Special Offer to the goldfish in their plastic bags of water. He was hoping to fool the old man into thinking that he was still toying with the idea of a goldfish, two, even. Then keeping his voice as steady as possible he said, 'And what are you asking for your Special Offer?'

'Remember that we won't be ripped-off,' said Clare, quickly. 'We know how you like to up the charge for the things you sell.'

The village children murmured their agreement. Felicity stamped her battered foot impatiently. She'd never had to bother about things costing a lot.

'Well, let's see if we can come to some fair agreement,' chuckled the old man. Turning the peak of his flat cap to the back of his head he addressed the crush of children in the ringing tones of a fairground barker. 'Okay, listen in, lovely little ladies and gentlemen, for I'm about to announce a Special Offer. For the absurdly low price of two bags of best-quality old woollens I am practically giving away this genuine dinosaur that you see tied to the back of my cart by a piece of string.'

There was a huge gasp from the children. At long last the object of their instant love had been named. And they had not been told false. For as dinosaurs went, the one that loomed high above them surely had to be the 'cracker' of crackers. His clawed feet were as big as small rubber dinghies. His curling scaly tail looked easily as long as a fun-fair train. His sinuous neck reared even higher than the poplar trees that lined both sides of the lane. As for his head perched on top of all that snaking neck, it was as comically small as it should be. He even wore, on his small pinched face, the proper sad expression. All this, plus his bright-green colour, matched him exactly with the dinosaurs the children were used to seeing on television. There was no doubt about it, the cracker of a dinosaur was genuine indeed. But what mystified everybody were the noises he made. He did not roar and bellow as they had expected. He muttered to himself. Because his head was so high up it was difficult to catch his actual words so the children could only guess and decided that the dinosaur was muttering, 'Dear, oh dear, oh dear,' to himself, while rolling his saucer-sized eyes in anguish. They had never heard such a cracker of a pet fret so. Not even their dogs still tied to the bench legs in the empty park could whine so piteously. But perhaps real flesh and blood dinosaurs always made a fuss about nothing? Was being completely miserable an important part of their character? Whatever the reason for all his moaning and groaning the children believed that a vigorous game of football in the park would soon bring the roses back to his cheeks and cheer him up. But that was a small problem for the future. Now the youngsters could only goggle upwards and marvel. Without words every child agreed that never had they seen anything so majestically lovely. They were determined that Tom and Clare should buy and free him.

What totally clinched their love for him was

his sudden, pathetic attempt at escape from the back of the old man's cart. Huge feet shuffling, he abruptly turned and tried to lumber through a gap in the hedge, only to pull up short when the tatty piece of string, that he could have easily broken, tautened around his huge neck. It seemed to the children, as they swallowed lumps in their throats, that the noble creature was more a prisoner of the mind than anything. Perhaps the prisoner of his own sad hopelessness. But it did cheer everyone up when the dinosaur at least showed a little spirit. As if to revenge himself for being unable to escape he swung down his head and nipped the tail of the old man's weary horse. Then he turned and popped two red balloons with his sharp front teeth. Then, observing that the old man was still grinning, the dinosaur returned to his passion – the chewing of the tops off poplar trees and muttering, 'Dear, oh dear, oh dear,' between mouthfuls.

But Saw Something Special

Felicity made the first move. . .

'I'll take your Special Offer,' she cried, dashing around to the back of the cart and fumbling at the string with busy fingers. 'I can easily pay you two bags of best-quality old woollens. Just don't let anyone touch him and I'll be back with the woollens before you know it, Rag-and-bone man.'

'You will not, Greenway,' fumed Tom, snatching the string from her eager hands. 'If the dinosaur belongs to anyone he belongs to Clare and me. Clare, hold this string tight while I negotiate.'

'The cheek,' cried Clare, wrapping the dinosaur's lead round her wrist and glaring at Felicity. 'Some people should learn to keep their greedy hands to themselves. Especially when they've got no old woollens on the spot like other people have.'

'Not enough, I'm afraid,' interrupted the old man, peering at the single bag Tom was offering. He realised that if he played his cards right he could make a lot more old woollens out of this angry situation. He went on, 'Of course, my goldfish offer is still open. Why not settle for one, two, even? Why not admit that you can't afford my Special Offer and let the posh little girl with the bird's-nest hairstyle have him?'

'How do you know the Prices can't afford the dinosaur?' demanded the boy who stood loyally next to Tom. His name was Tim and he was Tom's best mate. His family were very poor, which was why he was wearing a cast-off cashmere sweater that was much too tight all round. His usually shy eyes blazed angrily as he continued. 'How do you know the Prices can't get the extra old woollens? Why should everything nice always fall like a plum into Greenway's lap? Why does she need so many gears on her new bike when she never uses them?'

'Because I can afford nice things, that's why,' stormed Felicity. 'Anyway, the dinosaur will live a much better life with me. He will be spoiled rotten, for my dad owns most of the shops in this village and is rolling in money. As for Tom feeling sad about not owning a genuine dinosaur, well, he knows that he's always welcome to come for tea at Greenway Towers. And if he did he could take Greenie Greenway for a walk any time he chose.' To make her point clear she tried to link her arm through Tom's, only to be angrily pushed away.

'The nerve of some people,' gasped a girl who stood close to the tearful Clare. Her name was Jill and she was poor Tim's sister and also Clare's best friend. She was also Felicity's mortal enemy. Her eyes flashed fire as she launched into the pouting Greenway girl. 'How dare some people name a dinosaur they don't even own. How dare they invite people round to tea – people who wouldn't turn up in a million years.'

'I can do anything I like,' shouted Felicity, furiously. 'My dad told me so, and he should know with his pots of money.'

'Now hold on,' butted in the old man, his eyes gleaming greedily. 'I'm not sure even you can afford to buy my Special Offer, lovely little lady. I've just realised I've made a mistake. I've just remembered that three bags of best-quality old woollens is the going rate for a dinosaur in the peak of condition. But never mind if you can't afford him either. I'll see he finds a good home in the next village. What a pity nobody in this nice village can afford to buy the only one I've got left, and I don't know when I'll be getting in another batch, dinosaurs being so very scarce

21

these days. So can I interest you in something cheaper, spirited little lady? I've still got plenty of goldfish left. And if you'd like to change your mind about my balloons on a stick, get in quick, for my Special Offer seems determined to burst them all before he gets sold in the next village. No . . . I can't tempt you? Oh well, if one of you kiddies would tie my property to the end of my cart again. I'd hate him to escape before I reach my next port of call.'

A small boy stepped forward. He was known as Little Billy and was the best at maths in the whole village. He was also famous for being politely cheeky to parents, teachers, and even cunning rag-and-bone men. To cries of 'No' from the children packed into the bend in the lane he prized the dinosaur's string from Clare's white-knuckled hand and tied it back on the cart with a 'never-slip' scout's knot. The children were furious but they didn't dare stamp on his black polished shoes because they all needed to copy his answers to exam sums. Every single child was still determined that the dinosaur would never leave their village. The crafty rag-and-bone man knew that this Special Offer was as good as sold, though to whom, well, he couldn't have cared less. All he was interested in was driving the hardest bargain.

After checking to see that his valuable property was secure, he tugged on his reins, clicked to his horse and began to rumble up the lane, knowing quite well that the children would call him back.

'Dear, oh dear, oh dear,' murmured the shoved-around Special Offer shambling along behind, his huge mouth stuffed full of poplar-top. At that point he made another vain attempt to escape over the hedge. But the fragile string proved to be a strange and ridiculous barrier to his dinosaur way of thinking. So he contented his sore feelings by nipping the tail of the weary old horse again and maliciously bursting three more red balloons as he ambled along behind.

'Bring back that dinosaur,' yelled Felicity, stamping her battered trainers in a tantrum. She let go of Tom's T-shirt and raced to the front of the cart. Grabbing the tired old nag by its swinging feed-bag she shouted, 'Whoa, whoa,' and pushed with all her might, forcing the surprised creature back into the shafts. The horse was only too pleased to stop for another breather. After a mournful glance rearwards at his sore tail he plunged his nose into his meagre supply of oats and began to munch. A bit of grub relieved his tensions. Like any self-respecting horse he detested having to drag heavy dinosaurs around the countryside, especially moaning ones. As for Tom, although he always stoutly maintained that he hated Felicity as much as anyone, he couldn't help feeling a sneaking admiration for her. But he quickly pulled himself together. After all, Felicity was demanding the dinosaur even though she hadn't any old woollens to back her up.

'Changed your mind about the goldfish, determined little lady?' said the old man, his top set of teeth slipping down over the bottom set as he addressed her teasingly. 'Do you want me to wait while you run home for a large bag of old woollens?'

'No, I haven't changed my mind about your stupid old goldfish,' retorted Felicity. 'It's Greenie Greenway I want. That's why I'm ordering you to wait here until I return with three bags full. Not ordinary old woollens mind, I'll be bringing best-quality cashmere and Shetland that my mum usually gives away to poor children like Tim and Jill. Well, they'll have to go without for once. My Greenie Greenway is much more deserving. So, Mr Rag-and-bone man, don't budge an inch until I'm back.' And off she raced up the lane, her hair a wild mess, her stamped-on trainers flopping at the soles.

'You're not going to stand for that, Tom?' said Tim. He rounded on his stunned friend. 'You know what will happen if Greenway gets that dinosaur? She'll keep him locked away behind her dad's big iron gates and we'll never see him.'

'And we'll never hear the end of her spiteful boasting,' cried Jill to Clare, her cheeks as white as her second-hand Shetland woolly. 'She's bound to make the dinosaur's life even more miserable than it is. Just look at him chewing mournfully away on poplar-tops as if the weight of the world is on his enormous shoulders. How could he possibly learn to smile behind the iron bars of Greenway Towers? Ask Tom, he dreads the thought of only having to go to tea there. Imagine having to spend your whole life in such a place. So please, both of you, run home and beg your mother for two more bags of old woollens, before it's too late.'

'Why don't you all chip in and buy him between you?' asked the old man, puzzled. 'If you don't want that scruffy little rich girl to have him. Or am I mistaken about the mysterious ways of kids?'

'Of course you are,' scoffed Little Billy. 'You can't part-own a pet. It's either yours completely or it isn't yours at all. If we all chipped in with old socks and things, someone would have to work out exactly how much of the dinosaur each one owned, which would make everything very untidy. And guess who'd be lumbered with sorting out all the different shares into tidy columns? Me, of course, being the mathematical brains of the village. But I can't waste valuable exam-swatting time dividing up shares in a moaning dinosaur. It's hard enough having to waste my time whispering the answers to difficult sums to practically every kid here. No, Mr Rag-and-bone man, the ownership of your Special Offer dinosaur must be decided in a straight and tidy contest between the Prices and Felicity Greenway. I believe the Prices have first refusal. But I wonder if they've got the guts to fight for him? They look so defeated. By the way, did you know that whoever built your cart didn't know a thing about axle-stresses? According to the figures that I've just jotted down in my notebook that flimsy thing you are perched on should have collapsed under you long ago.'

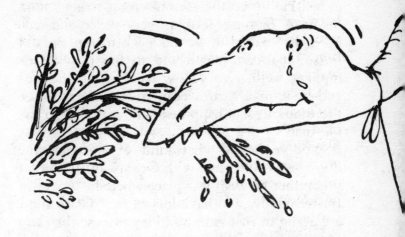

'Oh, shut up about your theories, Little Billy,' butted in Jill, impatiently. 'Your figures never make sense to us, anyway. What's at stake is the happiness of a flesh-and-blood dinosaur. And Tom will know what to do . . . but he'd better hurry, the Special Offer's weeping. It's as if the poor creature knows that Felicity Greenway is going to buy him and lock him up in her dad's big garden for ever.'

The children shaded their eyes to scrutinize the soaring giant. His eyes were certainly watering. But that could mean he was swallowing poplar-tops without chewing them first. He was moaning and groaning as usual as he cast around, tasting every bit of greenery within reach, muttering, 'Dear, oh dear, oh dear,' between gulps. He tested the cotton-strong string round his neck. Sighing, looking very vexed and red-eyed, he snaked down his neck to nip the old horse's backside again and to burst, with his nipping teeth, two yellow balloons on the rag-and-bone man's cart. Tom couldn't bear to see the dinosaur's unhappiness and appealed to the old man.

'You've heard what kind of existence the dinosaur would have with Greenway. Wouldn't you rather he went to a place where he would be treated kindly and have lots of fun? Clare and I are going to rush home and try to raise the extra old woollens. Will you wait and try not to sell him to anyone else until we return . . . please . . .?'

'Sorry,' replied the old man, ever the business executive. 'It's first come, first served in the rag-and-bone trade.'

Tom and Clare didn't wait to hear any more. With the encouraging cheers of their friends ringing in their ears they dashed for home, hell for leather. Meanwhile Tim and Jill organised the crowd of children into a menacing ring around the horse and cart and the moaning dinosaur to discourage the old man from moving so much as one clip-clop in the direction of the next village. This suited Little Billy perfectly. He settled down happily to jot down in his notebook more disturbing facts about the rickety cart for,

according to Archimedes, it was simply imposs-
ible for the vehicle to roll along with a huge
Special Offer dinosaur putting such a dragging
strain on its dodgy axles . . .

The Cost was High

'A dinosaur, eh?' said Mrs Price, her scatter-brained mind elsewhere. She was sitting in her cosy kitchen watching television and her washing-machine at the same time. Shifting her gaze from the quiz-show and the revolving family smalls she studied Tom and Clare through her red-tinted spectacles. 'I thought you two were mad for a goldfish, two, even? So why the change of heart? Especially when your father went to all that trouble and cleaned out the old bowl, and gritted his teeth over buying the concrete snail and the plastic weed from a Greenway shop. And you know very well that he'll be gritting his teeth again tonight to pick up some ants'-eggs from that loathsome man's place. Anyway, what do you want with a dinosaur?

Haven't you enough plastic rubbish cluttering up your bedrooms? I suppose you'll play with it for a few hours and then toss it aside like you did your Action Men and your Cabbage Patch dolls?'

'No, Mum, he's not a plastic dinosaur, he's a real one,' insisted Tom. 'He's all green and scaly and as tall as Dad's monkey-puzzle tree.'

'And he's got the saddest face,' breathed Clare. 'Wait till you see him, Mum, he'll break your heart too.'

'I'll bet that cunning old rag-and-bone man isn't breaking his heart,' said Mrs Price as she remembered when she was young and she'd had to settle for a balloon on a stick because goldfish cost too many old woollens for her poor family. She snorted. 'Three bags of old woollens for a plastic toy indeed. Oh, very well, if it will keep you from under my feet for a few hours, you can sort out all those expensive clothes you once begged for and won't wear now because they're out of fashion. By the way, you can throw in that old cardigan of your father's. Now that's something I will be glad to see the back of. Just remember to take the pipe out of the pocket.'

'We still won't have enough,' wailed Clare. 'And we've got to beat Felicity Greenway.'

'Can we have Patch's cuddling blanket, Mum?' said Tom inspired. 'You're always saying how it stinks to high heaven. We can always save up and buy him a new one.'

'You'd better ask Patch,' replied Mrs Price, turning back to the flickering plots on her portable television and washing-machine. 'But please, don't upset him. You know how his howling goes right through me.'

Tom and Clare didn't bother to ask the family dog what he thought about sacrificing his beloved blanket for a dinosaur. Instead, they tipped him howling from his basket in the living room and hastily stuffed his quilted woolly into a

32

plastic bag. After some more frantic searching they at last had enough old woollens to fill two bags. Lugging one apiece they raced out of the house and set off down the lane. To their relief they caught up with Felicity. She had easily gathered together her posh woollens, helped by her mother and the maid, the Greenways' 'little treasure'. However, Felicity's problem had been how to carry them. Daddy Greenway was out in the Rolls Royce collecting lots of money from his many shops, and because Mummy's almost-as-big car was still packed to the roof with dresses and shoes and presents for her adored

family, what could a desperate girl do? But spying her little brother happily tootling up and down the gravelled drive in his miniature red sports-car, she pounced. Chucking him out of it, she swiftly piled her bags of woollens aboard and, ignoring his screams, scooted down the drive for the lane. Soon she was trundling downhill towards the bend, swearing at the little car to make it go faster. Then her worst fears were confirmed. Glancing over her shoulder she saw the Prices gaining on her, their woollens bouncing on their backs, their breath coming in great gasps, their trainers relentlessly pounding the tarmac as they drew level with her. Cruelly, the toe of Tom's trainer thudded into the off-side wheel of the little red car, buckling it hopelessly and sending it careering into the ditch at the side of the lane. Caught off balance, Felicity, trying to hang on to her scattered bags of woollens, also came a cropper in the muddy ditch. Tom couldn't resist looking over his shoulder. He had to admire Felicity, valiantly dragging her woollens from the ditch, but not for long. All at once he and Clare were in sight of the bend in the lane and romping home the winners.

'So you won then?' said the rag-and-bone man, looking disappointed. He had had visions of his large brood of grandchildren proudly pulling on Felicity's cashmere and Shetland sweaters. But glancing around the crowd of children, who still hemmed him into the bend in the lane, he knew that any treachery on his part was out of the question.

As for the dinosaur, ignoring the cheers for the winners he continued to moan, 'Dear, oh dear, oh dear,' while tackling the prickly problem of a holly-bush snack.

'We have honoured our part of the agreement, will you honour yours?' gasped Tom, trying to get his wind back.

'Can we untie the dinosaur and take him home now?' wheezed Clare, grateful for Jill's healing pats on her back. 'Here are the extra two bags of old woollens making three in all.'

For proof the bags were hoisted aboard his cart by the happy children. All eyes were fixed intently on the old man as he opened one up and inspected the contents. He seemed satisfied.

'Nice bit of stuff,' he remarked, fingering Patch's cuddling blanket. 'Pongs a bit, but yes, the Special Offer dinosaur can now change hands. Untie him by all means. I expect you're anxious to rush him off for a game of football in the park.'

All the children sighed with relief. At last the wheeling and dealing was over. At last the cracker of a dinosaur belonged to the right people, Tom and Clare . . . and themselves a little. For they knew that the generous Prices would gladly allow any of them to take their new pet on an outing. Something that the hated Felicity would never permit. Yes, the children were much looking forward to 'dinosaur-walking' as opposed to the dreaded 'poodle-walking' they were required to do by certain old ladies with bad legs.

So it was with a feeling of sharing that they watched the Prices lovingly free their new pet from the back of the old man's cart. The dinosaur tested the tautness of the string, as he eyed the gap in the hedge. But realising that he was now tethered by four firm hands he returned to his moaning and groaning and gulping down the holly-bush he had torn from the ground, his 'Dear, oh dear, oh dears' loud on the summer air. But the children were certain that with lots of love and plenty of brisk games, the miserable dinosaur would soon be smiling his head off. For his future was now in the right hands. Just then a thought occurred to practical Clare.

'I've just realised,' she said. 'You didn't tell us his name. He does have a name, I suppose?'

'Well, for what it's worth I call him Old Grumble,' replied the old man with a smile. Having got rid of the dinosaur he could insult him now. 'And I think you'll find it a most suitable name, for he's done nothing but moan and groan from the moment I tied him to the back of my cart. But then what do you expect for three bags of old woollens? One thing is certain, you can't buy a sense of humour. But hello, here comes our scruffy little friend. I wonder if she'd be willing to swap those quality old woollens for a balloon on a stick, two, even, plus two gold-fish, three, even . . ?'

'Cheats, thieves,' screamed Felicity. She came scooting up in her brother's battered red car, her bags of woollens piled high. Though blinking back tears she was defiant as ever and to Tom she looked even prettier. Ignoring the mocking village children and the old man she confronted the winners. Tom and Clare jealously guarded their dinosaur.

'What do you mean, "cheats"?' said Tom, indignantly. 'It was a fair race with no holds barred. Under the rules of the contest, we won our dinosaur fair and square.'

'Do you call that fair?' yelled Felicity, grabbing hold of his T-shirt sleeve and pointing angrily at the car's buckled wheel. 'I was miles in front coming down the lane until you sabotaged me. So if you want to be fair, hand over Greenie Greenway to me at once. If you don't I'll tell my dad and he'll come and tow your dad's used-car back to the Greenway Auto Showrooms. It's a wonder he hasn't before, he's always complaining about how far behind your dad is with his payments. In fact, my dad says that your dad is nothing but a cheapskate!'

'Don't you talk about our dad like that,

Greenway,' bristled Tom. 'Anyway my dad thinks your dad is nothing but a fat money-grabber with no class. And who said you could call our new pet Greenie Greenway?'

'As if he was one of your shops,' echoed Clare, angrily.

'Like you'd like to own Tom himself,' said Jill, flushing with jealousy.

'And don't look daggers at Clare like that,' spoke up Tim, blushing to the roots of his hair.

'I can say and do what I like,' Felicity flared. But all at once she was appealing to Tom. 'If you like me as much as I think you do, please hand

me my dinosaur, Tom.'

'But Tom doesn't like you,' said Jill, smugly.
'He's said so often enough, but you never seem
to hear. And what's more, if Tom should decide
on a new name for his new pet I'll bet it won't be
anything so childish as Greenie Greenway.'

'The dinosaur's name should have a "Price" on
the end,' butted in Little Billy, crawling from
beneath the old man's cart where he'd been
shaking his head at the lack of fulcrum and
balance. He took off his spectacles and polished
the oil from them. 'Now if Tom and Clare
decide to call him something dignified like
'Newton Faraday', their new pet's full name
would be Newton Faraday Price. In that way
everyone would know clearly who he belonged
to. It's a bit like sums really. If a family are called
X, then there's never the danger of them being
confused with a family called Y and causing Pi to
go haywire. It's simple really.'

'No, Little Billy,' interrupted Clare. She gazed
up at the Special Offer. 'Things to do with love
are never simple. I think we'll call him . . .' her
lips moved soundlessly as she considered. Then
her face lit up. 'I know, because he is used to it
he'll be "Grumble". But because he is so very
sweet his full name will be Dear Grumble.'

'Dear Grumble "Price",' corrected Little Billy,
scribbling down the new name in his notebook.
'Otherwise everyone will get into a terrible

mathematical quandary. And guess who will have to sort it all out? Not that I'd mind too much . . .'

'Dear Grumble Price.' The other children weren't impressed. Some of them felt more inclined towards 'Godzilla' or something equally romantic. 'Dear Grumble Price' himself seemed instantly bored by his new name. He didn't even glance down when Clare softly addressed him by it. Cutting her dead, he chewed away on a blackberry bush he'd ripped from the ground, his 'dear, oh dear, oh dears' as plaintive as before. Obviously there were many in the bend in the lane who were dubious about the Prices' choice. But, as the legal owners, Tom and Clare were entitled to call their pea-green giant any silly thing they chose. And then it was time for everyone to leave the bend in the lane. But not before the rag-and-bone man had made his last appeal to the fuming Felicity.

'About those old woollens,' he said, pointing at the piled-up red car. 'It's a pity to have to lug 'em all the way home again. So what say we make some sort of deal? How about if you give 'em me now on a promise that next time I call I'll bring you a dolly that cries "Mama", and wets herself each time you press her stomach? Now I can't say fairer than that . . .'

'Keep your crying and wetting dollies, I've got a whole cupboard-full of them at home,' shrilled

41

Felicity, weeping and stamping both battered feet. She shook a warning finger. 'And I haven't forgotten what you said about not knowing when you'll be having another batch of dinosaurs in. Just remember that when you do you'd better put one exactly like Greenie Greenway aside, for me, just in case the Prices don't give me back what's rightfully mine. If you don't, my dad will come and visit you in his big Rolls Royce with the spanner he keeps in the glove compartment. Do you understand, Rag-and-bone man?'

'Perfectly, little lady,' said the old man, shifting uncomfortably in his seat on the cart. Hurriedly he called his goodbyes to the children.

'Nice doing business with you. I hope you have many happy hours playing ball and going for walks with that cracker of a dinosaur.' Then with a tug on his reins and a click to his horse he trundled away on his shaky-wheeled cart up the lane.

'If that cart makes it to the next village it will be a miracle,' said a grave Little Billy. 'Apart from his axle trouble, the shafts of that cart are not correctly aligned along the longitudinal angle of his directional plane. But then, what do rag-and-bone men care about the disaster of not knowing that the sums of squares should be equal to adjacent sides? But then, what do you lot care for, except trivia and my accurate sums to copy? Tell you one thing, I'm not going to end up bagging-up goldfish or be a pop-star. I've already written a letter to Space Control at Cape Canaveral . . .'

'Oh, shut up about your wild ambitions, Little Billy,' chorused the village children. Though they liked him and he was one of the gang, they only really listened to him during school hours. Anyway, the only ambition they had on this fine summer-holiday morning was to lead Dear Grumble up the lane to his new home and life at the Prices'.

They set off in procession up the hill. Tom and Clare made sure that every child held Dear Grumble's string for at least a few yards. Even Felicity was allowed a turn. She managed to annoy everyone by looking up at Dear Grumble all the time and whispering, 'Don't you wish you were coming home with me, dear Greenie Greenway?' But the dinosaur didn't seem to care whose home he was going to. So long as the children occasionally slackened their grip on his string so that he could snake out his head and crop the tops off poplar trees, he didn't spare them so much as a glance. He merely shambled obediently behind whoever happened to be leading him. And all the while he never stopped his anguished eye-rolling and his miserable 'dear, oh dearing' all the way up the lane. Tom was in poor spirits also. To think that as part owner he had yet to have a turn at leading Dear Grumble home.

'Why is Tom pushing Felicity's bags of old woollens up the hill in that silly red car?' said Jill, looking flustered and indignant. 'Especially when she is having the fun of leading Dear Grumble.'

'It's called blackmail,' said Little Billy, wisely. 'Put simply, if someone you try to avoid threatens to hold your hand unless you push their red racing-car up a lane, then you do it. It's all to do with Biology. Do you know what the black-widow spider does to her mate . . .?'

'We don't want another lecture, Little Billy,' said Clare firmly. 'And if you're interested, it's your turn on Dear Grumble's string.' Little Billy was off like a shot. Meanwhile, at the back, Tom puffed and panted as he pushed the buckled red car up the hill. He had to admit that Felicity, leading Dear Grumble, her wild blonde hair streaming in the wind, her trainers flapping at the soles, was a most attractive sight.

Dear Grumble showed no sign of excitement when Clare pointed out the small semi-detached that would be his new home for ever and a day. He did look gloomily interested when he spied the tall monkey-puzzle tree that grew in the centre of Mr Price's immaculate garden. At last, Tom and Clare could race indoors to drag their mother from her television and washing-machine and beg her to come outside to see their new pet. They need not have bothered, Mrs Price had heard the commotion in the road outside her front door and had peered through her lace curtains to see what was going on.

'What in heaven's name,' she murmured, clutching at her heart. Her agitation was justi-fied. It was bad enough seeing the village chil-dren perched like starlings along Mr Price's new fence but it was the huge green object tied to the gate that caused her to feel faint and chew nervously on her red-painted fingernails. Could it be a bulldozer or a crane that the council workmen had left outside the house while they went for a pint of beer in the Greenway Arms? But if so, why was it eyeing Mr Price's prized monkey-puzzle tree as if preparing to eat it down to the ground? In her flustered state Mrs Price began to imagine all kinds of things. She confided in Patch, who had his front paws on the sill beside her, as he too stared anxiously out of the window.

'Could it be a hot-air balloon, Patch?' she whispered. 'You know, the sort that margarine people use to promote their product? Or could it be the *Blue Peter* team up to one of their japes? So where are the cameras, the microphones, the lights. And just look at the state of my hair. I couldn't possibly go on camera with my red highlights looking like rat's-tails.'

Patch whined and stared up the garden path. He wasn't trying to fool himself like his mistress. He saw the dinosaur for what it was.

'Perhaps you, too, will be appearing on television, Patch,' said Mrs Price, chewing her nails and clutching at straws. 'If it is the *Blue Peter* team they always have dogs on their programme.'

The small, liver-spotted dog's whine became a despairing howl. He had watched *Blue Peter* as often as anyone in the Price household. Like every dog in the land he had always fancied being sat on a comfy cushion in the studio, a *Blue Peter* badge pinned to his collar. But Patch was more wise to the ways of the world than Mrs Price. He knew that what he was staring at was a huge

46

green dinosaur that could well cook his goose as chief pet to the Price family.

'Well, one thing is certain, Patch,' said Mrs Price, still refusing to accept the truth. 'If those council people think they can park their junk outside this house then they've got another think coming. Come on, let's sort this out before Mr Price comes home and flies up the wall.'

It was with feelings of deep dread that Patch slunk close to the red-slippered heels of his mistress as she marched to the front door to confront her excited children who were haring down the path towards her. Mrs Price was luckier than Patch. She had her red-painted nails to chew on in moments of crisis. But the old and faithful family pet had no such comfort now that he'd lost his favourite cuddling shawl. As he followed her, what had been a whine and then a howl became the full-blooded cry of a wolf in dire straits.

But They Raced Home to Raise it

'Who told the council they could park their earth-moving equipment outside your father's front gate?' cried Mrs Price, shooing her babbling children back up the path. 'And if it's a *Blue Peter* film crew, tell them that I won't have their bright lights shining in my eyes.'

'But it isn't council property, Mum. Nor is it anything to do with *Blue Peter*,' shouted Tom, his eyes shining. 'Don't you remember us saying that we were trying to raise enough old woollens to buy a dinosaur from the rag-and-bone man? Well, we did. So aren't you pleased to know that you are part-owner of our new pet?'

'You did your bit by throwing in Dad's old cardigan,' said Clare, happily.

'I don't believe this,' said Mrs Price, burying

her face in her plastic apron, not caring that Patch had been trying to do the same. Imploringly she whispered in a muffled voice, 'Please tell me that you are up to your tricks. Please tell me that the monstrosity tied to your father's front gate is a hot-air balloon that will float away at any minute.'

'Our Dear Grumble will never float away, we promise, Mum,' said Clare, firmly. 'He is here to stay in our happy home for ever.'

'So the council won't be coming to collect it?' sobbed Mrs Price, her nerves, like Patch's, in tatters. 'And the *Blue Peter* team is a figment of my imagination . . .?'

'*Blue Peter*?' said Tom, puzzled. 'Why should they be interested in our small village? What's the matter, Mum, don't you like our new pet?'

Mrs Price removed the plastic apron from her face. She was close to breakdown as her red-tinted eyes took in the huge bulk of Dear Grumble, who was moaning as usual. Faintly she said, 'But I thought you two had set your heart on a goldfish, two, even? And can you tell those friends of yours to get down from your father's new fence and gate. You know how much trouble he took putting it up and screwing on those hinges.'

'Never mind Dad's gate, Mum,' said Tom, urgently. 'Just look at Dear Grumble. We couldn't possibly take him back. The rag-and-bone man will be well on his way to the next village by now. So what do you think about our real dinosaur? Don't you think he puts the one in *The Fintstones* to shame?'

'And didn't you fall in love with him at first sight?' breathed Clare, gazing fondly upwards. 'And don't you think that Dad will too?'

'How can anyone fall in love with a real dinosaur at first sight?' wept Mrs Price, raising her red-tinted eyes skywards. 'Especially one with a face like a wet weekend. And why does it keep muttering, 'Dear, oh dear, oh dear'? And why is it sniffing at your father's monkey-puzzle tree as

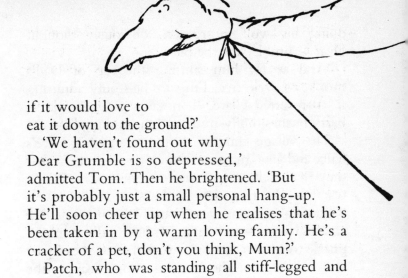

if it would love to
eat it down to the ground?'
    'We haven't found out why
Dear Grumble is so depressed,'
admitted Tom. Then he brightened. 'But
it's probably just a small personal hang-up.
He'll soon cheer up when he realises that he's
been taken in by a warm loving family. He's a
cracker of a pet, don't you think, Mum?'
    Patch, who was standing all stiff-legged and

doing his wolf impression, obviously thought Dear Grumble was the pits.

'And as for him sniffing the top of Dad's monkey-puzzle tree, I'm sure he's only admiring it,' comforted Clare. 'Dinosaurs only eat black-berry bushes, holly-trees, and the odd poplar-top.'

The village children, strung along Mr Price's fence and gate, murmured their agreement. At first they had felt apprehensive about Mrs Price's reaction. But now they could relax. If all she was worried about was Dear Grumble's miserable face and his harmless interest in her husband's monkey-puzzle tree, then they were sure she could easily be won round. For the first time since leaving the bend in the lane they cheered, a few slipping down from their perch to pat Dear Grumble about his huge ankles. Dear Grumble was not the slightest bit moved by yet another display of affection. He continued to murmur his 'dear, oh dear, oh dears' to himself as he flicked out his gigantic tongue and delicately explored Mr Price's monkey-puzzle tree for taste.

Little Billy was equally unmoved by all the sentiment. His world revolved around the truth and long columns of figures. Yet he was an amiable lad. He didn't mind when the other children ribbed him about his habit of arriving for school before the teachers. Nor did he take offence when they teased him for wearing his school cap and blazer during the summer holidays, his top pocket stuffed with his notebook and coloured biros. While all the argy-bargy had been going on, he had been studying the hinges on Mr Price's new gate. He was trying to work out with a biro and notebook how such cheap hinges could possibly support the weight of so many swinging children. But he felt obliged to give his considered opinion about the monkey-tree puzzle. He was not reassuring.

'Clare is right but only up to a point,' he said. 'Anyone can see that Dear Grumble is suffering from some deep stress known only to himself. I believe that sooner or later he will crack, and when he does he'll take it out on the thing closest to him – Mr Price's monkey-puzzle tree. And when he's scoffed that one his nerves will probably force him to charge about the village in search of other monkey-puzzle trees to digest. For it's a well-known fact that unhappy people often stuff themselves with junk-food to make themselves feel better. Dear Grumble is probably a classic case.'

'Is that little boy really as wise as they say?' said Mrs Price, weakly. 'Mr Price won't be amused to hear his beloved tree described as junk-food. Oh dear, and what's the huge green monster doing now . . . .?'

Dear Grumble had suddenly swooped down his head to snatch up Little Billy by the seat of his smart school pants. The children and Mrs Price watched in astonishment as Billy was swung over their heads and then dropped from the height of about ten feet into the rose-bed of Mrs Lovejoy next door. Then Dear Grumble returned to staring moodily at the top of the monkey-puzzle tree, murmuring, 'Dear, oh dear, oh dear.'

'I wonder why Dear Grumble did that?' gasped Tom. 'Apart from nipping the old man's horse, our new pet is usually so non-violent.'

'Little Billy brought it on himself,' said Clare, defensively. 'Didn't you notice that when he was accusing Dear Grumble of being a junk-food addict he was tapping Dear Grumble's toenail with his biro? Anyway, Little Billy isn't hurt. Here he comes from next door now . . .'

'It was my own fault,' said Little Billy, generously. He winced and rubbed his stung backside. 'That's the last time I'll scribble down notes on Dear Grumble's toenail. Now where was I . . .?'

'You were saying how unhappy Greenie Greenway is,' shouted Felicity, seizing her chance. 'And if it's junk-food he needs then I can provide him with all he wants.'

'What's that Greenway girl doing shouting and stamping her feet in your father's geranium-bed?' frowned Mrs Price.

'I am trying to get back what rightfully

54

belongs to me,' Felicity yelled. She stamped her battered trainer into Mr Price's flowers again. 'I demand that you let me lead him up to Greenway Towers. I'll soon calm his nerve problem. My dad owns The Greenway Fast-Food Nookery in the High Street and he'll see that Greenie has plenty of triple-decker burgers and hot-dogs dripping with tomato sauce and all the chips he can eat. If my Greenie was allowed to come home with me he would never need to lick his chops over a tasteless monkey-puzzle tree that looks half dead anyway.'

'Why does the little hussy refer to our . . . to your dinosaur as "Greenie"?' enquired Mrs Price, patting the whining Patch on his dry nose.

Jill seized her chance. Because she was too kind to smack Felicity's face for pulling Tom's T-shirt about, she took her revenge by telling true tales. Flushed with anger she said, 'It's because Felicity won't accept that Dear Grumble belongs to your children, Mrs Price. Being so spoiled she insists that they won him unfairly from the rag-and-bone man. So please, Mrs Price, let Tom and Clare keep him for we are all fed-up with Felicity's dad giving her everything she wants so that she can flaunt it in our faces.'

The children, strung out along the gate and fence, clapped vigorously. Mrs Price agreed.

'As far as I'm concerned Dear Grumble is welcome to live here as long as he wants,' she announced. 'And that goes for Mr Price too, I'm sure. So, young lady, I'll thank you to take your feet out of our geraniums and get back to the other side of our fence where you belong.'

The loud hurrah that greeted her stand quickly died away as marching up next-door's path came the dreaded Mrs Lovejoy. She always had to poke her nose into things that didn't concern her. Elbowing her way through the crush of children she folded her arms over her chest and angrily addressed Mrs Price. 'I hope that dinosaur isn't going to stay parked there all night,' she said, grimly. 'And don't tell me it's a council bulldozer or a hot-air balloon, for I watch enough television to know a dinosaur when I see one.'

'We'll park our dinosaur anywhere we want,' flared back Mrs Price. 'My children are entitled to have a pet if they want one.'

'Not a pet that blocks out the light,' Mrs Lovejoy snapped. 'I hope you realise that my goldfish likes to watch the sun go down from his bowl in my window? But then your rough children probably don't care a fig about gentle goldfish like my Goldie. I saw them sitting on the gate with their woollens this morning. So why didn't they settle for a balloon on a stick or a lovely fish like my Goldie, two, even? But no, they had to have that great lumbering monstrosity. Well, Mrs Price, I just hope you intend to get rid of him, and as soon as possible. I warn you, if he's not gone by the morning I'll be down to complain to the council quicker than you can say "blink".'

'Don't you call my children "rough",' shouted Mrs Price. 'Who do you think you are, trying to tell us what to do with our own dinosaur? Well, let me tell you this, our Dear Grumble is here to stay. And my husband will tell you the same . . . I think. And here he comes home from work right now. He'll soon clear this matter up.'

Hurriedly the children scrambled down from the fence and gate as Mr Price came tootling

down the road in his new, second-hand car. As a rule Mr Price always arrived home at six-fifteen on the dot. But because he had stopped to buy a packet of ants'-eggs, he was five minutes late. And Mr Price hated to be late for anything, which explained why he was in a hurry and not looking exactly where he was going. When he saw a dinosaur tied to his front gate he swerved wildly, instantly lost control of his car and smashed it straight through his fence.

'I suppose you've noticed the dinosaur tied to

your gate, Mr Price?' fumed Mrs Lovejoy, running to peer in through the driver's window. 'I hope you intend to get rid of it by the morning, because if you don't I will be down to see the council like a shot.'

'I'm not completely blind, Mrs Lovejoy,' groaned Mr Price through his split lip. He sat in a bewildered daze as Tom, Clare and Mrs Price feverishly unfastened him from his seat-belt and helped him from the wreck. Soon he was hobbling up the drive, gratefully clinging on to the arm of his concerned wife.

'You did hear me say a dinosaur?' shrilled Mrs Lovejoy. 'I'm not talking about a piece of earth-moving equipment or a hot-air balloon, you know. What I'm talking about is a real-live monster with a face like a boiled haddock.'

'I do watch *The Fintstones*, Mrs Lovejoy,' said a badly-shaken Mr Price over his shoulder. 'If you'll just allow me to limp indoors and collect my senses.'

'Thank heaven you didn't crash into Dear Grumble, Dad,' said a relieved Tom as he took his father's other arm and helped him over the front doorstep.

'Too right,' chimed Clare shuddering, her strong hands pushing her father from behind. 'If Dear Grumble had been run over, he'd have been even more depressed. If you, his father figure, damaged him for no reason at all, he'd have been warped for life.'

'Never mind about the dinosaur, just attend to my damages,' said Mr Price, reeling dizzily against the door-jamb. Then his mind began to wander a bit. 'It was a dinosaur I ran into, wasn't it? And I have wrecked my car that I haven't finished paying for, haven't I? And is it my fancy, but was that monster gazing at my monkey-puzzle tree in a hungry manner? He's not going to eat it, is he? I've had that tree from a young sapling.'

'Dear Grumble probably will if his nervous system packs up, Mr Price,' shouted Little Billy up the path. 'And when he does, they'll probably send out a *Blue Peter* team to cover it. Then you will become as famous in our village as Mr Greenway. And perhaps richer, too, if you get invited on to Chat and Quiz-shows.'

'Shut your mouth, you cheeky little devil,' yelled Mr Price. 'If you aren't careful I'll be having a chat with your father about you. I know where you live. And stop fiddling with the hinges on my gate. And . . . oh, goodness, just look at the state of my fence.'

'Later, dear, later,' soothed Mrs Price, herding him and her children and Patch inside the house, and firmly shutting the door on the crazy world outside.

To Buy the Most Miserable Pet in the World

The living room was strangely quiet that evening. There was no television watching that tea-time. The *T.V. Times* remained unthumbed. The Price family were experiencing something rare indeed. Namely, a row without the goggle-box intruding. And a public row too, for the village children and the nosy Mrs Lovejoy were still hanging about outside, their ears straining to catch every angry word.

'What do you mean, goldfish are boring?' shouted Mr Price. 'At least a goldfish, two, even, wouldn't be blocking up most of the road outside. So where is this Dear Grumble planning to live, I'd like to know? And don't say my front garden. There's barely room enough for my monkey-puzzle tree as it is.'

'That's no problem, Dad,' said Tom who had been thinking about just that. 'As we no longer have a garden fence Dear Grumble can live with his back portion curled along the pavement and his front half wrapped around your tree.'

'And as you will probably have to sell your car for scrap, Dear Grumble can snake his head into your empty garage when he gets cramp,' said Clare, excitedly. 'So water won't trickle down his neck if it rains.'

'No way,' cried Mr Price, wincing as his wife applied a plaster to his split lip. He then posed another question. 'Anyway, we could never afford to feed him. What does the great lump eat, apart from everything in sight . . . including my tree if he gets the chance?'

'Dear Grumble's diet is no problem, Dad,' said Clare, confidently. 'He's quite happy to tuck into blackberry bushes, holly-boughs, and the odd poplar-top. So you need never worry that he'll sneak his head through the window and dig into your personal box of After Eight mints like Patch does. Even Tom and I wouldn't dare to do that.'

'And as for your monkey-puzzle tree, we plan to take him for long walks in the park,' said Tom. 'Plenty of fresh air will keep his nerves on an even keel, and then if we also show him lots of love I reckon he'll soon be as well-adjusted as you, Dad.'

'Well-adjusted?' laughed Mr Price, hysterically.

'I'll soon be well-adjusted in prison if that monster gets a crack at the Green Belt. The Conservationists will have my hide. By the way, it's getting a bit nippy in here. Where's my old cardigan? Look, Patch is shivering too. Come to think of it, where's his favourite cuddling shawl?'

'Ah now, Dad,' said Tom, solemnly. 'If we wish to own a cracker of a pet like Dear Grumble, we must all make small sacrifices. And don't forget because of what you've contributed you are now part-owner of him. Aren't you glad, Dad? I'm sure Patch is.'

'We did rescue your pipe from the pocket,' said Mrs Price, forgetting the split lip, and shoving the stem into her husband's mouth.

For a long while Mr Price spluttered as if searching for a way to blow his top without swearing. Eager to share his master's distress Patch slunk across from his basket and buried his hot dry nose in Mr Price's trouser pocket. At last Mr Price found the right words but before he could really get going, Mrs Price butted in to defend her children.

'Oh very well,' she said, crossly. 'If you've made up your mind that Dear Grumble must go we'll let the little Greenway madam have him. She's waiting outside in the hope that you'll do just that. Why should you care tuppence if his name is changed from Dear Grumble to Greenie Greenway?'

'What?' bawled Mr Price, sitting bolt upright in his armchair, his face like thunder. 'So those jumped-up crooks are poking their noses in our private business, eh? Isn't it enough that they own almost all the village? And now they're trying to get their sticky fingers on our new pet . . . I mean our children's new pet. Well, let me

tell you this . . .'

'What are you trying to splutter, dear?' asked Mrs Price, innocently.

'I know,' exulted Tom, punching the air with happiness. 'He's trying to splutter that Dear Grumble will be banished to Greenway Towers over his dead body.'

'I knew Dad would side with us,' said Clare, wiping away a tear. 'Even at the risk of losing his monkey-puzzle tree which is half-dead anyway.'

'That's enough, young lady,' Mr Price snapped. 'Exotic trees always look parched and droopy. Anyway, it's not that I want the nuisance of a dinosaur but I'm not going to let those grasping Greenways get him.'

'Which is your father's way of saying that he's beginning to like Dear Grumble very much,' said Mrs Price, dryly. 'Though I doubt if it means that he will be taking him for a walk in the park. Down the pub on Sunday morning, maybe, eh dear?'

But Tom and Clare planned to do that themselves. As for taking Dear Grumble pub-crawling on Sunday mornings, he could take Patch as he always did. Of course, no one asked the dog for his opinion. If they had they would have learned that Patch hated hanging around pubs while his master drank lots of pints of beer. He would have much preferred to go for walks in the park with Tom and Clare. But also, the arrival of his hated rival had dashed those hopes forever. Whimpering his protests, he slunk back to his basket, hopped inside and sullenly played dead . . .

Just then the Prices were startled to hear the blaring of a car-horn. Mr Price's bruised face darkened. He knew the sound of that horn very well. A deep, rich, melodious sound, it belonged to the most expensive Rolls Royce . . .

'If he's come to cause trouble he'll get it,' snarled Mr Price, limping to the front door and flinging it open. 'I'll give him blasting his horn outside my house.'

It was Mr Greenway right enough. He was just getting out of his Roller, a big bag of money chained to his wrist. Instantly Felicity flew across to sob and babble into his sharp three-piece suit. Mrs Lovejoy zoomed across to join them. Soon she was also bending Mr Greenway's ear, pointing now and again at the Prices standing in their doorway. By this time the village children could scarcely contain their excitement. The crowning event of the day would be a fight between Mr Price and Mr Greenway.

'Dear, oh dear, oh dear,' murmured Dear Grumble, his own attention firmly somewhere else.

'They did what? They pinched what?' bellowed Mr Greenway, running back to his car and snatching a spanner from the glove compartment.

67

Hefting it he marched through the Prices' smashed fence and stood glowering, his feet planted disrespectfully in the geranium-bed. Then, suddenly cautious, he placed the spanner between his knees and fumbled in his coat for his dark glasses which he promptly donned.

'Who told you to come charging into my garden?' shouted Mr Price. 'And I'll thank you to take your big feet out of my geraniums.'

'Never mind about your Bill-and-Ben garden,' Mr Greenway yelled back. 'Just tell those ruffian kids of yours to give my little Flick her dinosaur back. She thinks the world of . . . what's his name, love?'

'Greenie Greenway, Papa,' whimpered Felicity. 'And they stamped on my trainers and pulled my hair.'

'Not only theft but common assault too,' said Mr Greenway, disbelievingly. 'I hope you realise this is a police matter, Price? I think my little Flick is owed an apology as well as her dinosaur back. And tell your kids to be quick about it. Otherwise I'll drive down to the police station and have a word with an inspector friend of mine.'

'Does that mean I'll have to go to prison, Dad?' whispered Tom, suddenly frightened.

'And me into a convent?' sniffed Clare, clinging to her mother.

'Over your father's dead body, dears,'

68

comforted Mrs Price. 'Right is on our side. Leave it to your dad, he'll sort it out.'

'Threaten my kids again and I'll be up this path to you, Greenway,' warned Mr Price.

'Yes, well, your kind would know all about violence,' sneered Mr Greenway, pushing his glasses firmly on his nose and gripping his spanner tight.

'You can talk,' Mr Price scoffed. 'What's the spanner for then? To mend my car? It's a pity you didn't service it properly before it left your forecourt. It can't hold the road for toffee. So what do you intend to do about it? I'm thinking of calling in the law myself.'

'What do you expect for what you paid for it?' shouted Mr Greenway. 'If you are cheap, you buy cheap. But I'm not here to cry over your car. I'm here to see that justice is done to my little Flick. So are your kids going to hand Greenie Greenway back or not?'

'They are not,' gritted Mr Price, advancing a few steps up the path. He waved his pipe at the other man. 'My children bought this dinosaur fair and square. Is it their fault that your daughter was brought up to believe that she can have everything she sets her eyes on? Well, this time she can't.'

Felicity stood on tip-toe to whisper into her father's ear. Mr Greenway straightened and cleared his throat.

'My little Flick is prepared to overlook the theft,' he said. 'She has generously offered to give your kids the three bags of woollens stacked on her brother's red car. In return they must give her Greenie Greenway. We can't say better than that, considering she was cheated out of him in the first place. However, if it's money you want . . . Poorer people usually do.'

'Tell him to go and choke on his smoked salmon,' cried the furious Mrs Price. 'I think we've had quite enough of the Greenway charm for one day.'

'I'll choke him myself,' fumed Mr Price. He then addressed the smug Mr Greenway, his angry voice raised and echoing up and down the road. But he didn't care, he was so angry. 'Do you think you can buy our Dear Grumble for a paltry three bags of woollens? That wouldn't even pay for one hair on his miserable head. There is one thing you will never be able to throw a wad of notes at, and that's my children's Dear Grumble. Now get out of my geranium-bed before I set Patch on you. And, by the way, I'm still not satisfied with that car you sold me.'

'Is that your last word, Price?' shouted Mr Greenway. 'Very well, but you'll be hearing from my legal people before long.'

At this point Little Billy butted in. He had been walking round and round Mr Price's battered car, notebook in hand as he examined it minutely.

'Now, lad, what are you messing about with this time?' said Mr Price, irritably. 'Haven't you seen a car before?'

'Of course I have, Mr Price,' replied Little Billy. 'But this is the first time I've seen two halves of two different cars welded together. I'm afraid the man who sold you this must have seen you coming, Mr Price.'

'I should have guessed it,' Mr Price raged. 'That's why it wouldn't hold the road properly. I've paid good money for a codged-up old banger with a lick of new paint to cover up the joins. Right, Greenway, you aren't the only one who'll be consulting his legal people.'

'Try that and I'll bankrupt you, if you aren't already,' roared Mr Greenway. 'We'll see whose money talks the loudest. Come along Flick, love.'

Turning abruptly, he stormed out of Mr Price's geranium-bed and began to load the bags of woollens and the little red car into the spacious boot of his Rolls Royce. Meanwhile Felicity had run down the path to tug at Tom's T-shirt and to whisper some weepy words into his ear only he could hear. Then leaving him blushing she ran back to the car to be driven away to Greenway Towers. The village children cheered themselves hoarse to see them go. They cheered louder when Mrs Lovejoy marched back indoors to feed Goldie his ants'-eggs.

'Well, that's put paid to them,' said Mrs Price, her eyes gleaming with satisfaction behind her red-tinted spectacles. 'They'll think twice before they come demanding and complaining outside our house again. And now I think I'll go and warm up our television-suppers in my microwave. Will you warm up the telly, dear?'

'I think I'll go straight up to bed,' said Mr Price, looking completely drained. 'Thank heaven it's Saturday tomorrow and I can have a nice lie in.'

'Yes, well you have suffered a series of shocks,' said Mrs Price, kindly. 'But I'm proud of the stand you took, dear. So off to bed with you. Take my portable television up with you in case you can't sleep and want to watch the late horror movie. I'll be up with your supper in a few minutes. It's curried chicken and rice tonight which I know you love. Come on.' Tenderly she helped him to limp back into the house.

In the meantime the village children seemed reluctant to go home for their own suppers. They felt they just had to express the triumph that bubbled restlessly inside them, and to share in the happiness Tom and Clare must be feeling. They were not disappointed. With wide smiles on their faces Tom and Clare walked up the path to more loud cheers. Tom held up his hand for quiet.

'Did we waste our old woollens on a balloon on a stick?' he shouted.

'Not likely,' chorused the children.

'And did we throw away our woollens on a goldfish, two, even?' cried Clare.

'Goldfish, how boring,' scoffed the children, grimacing.

'So what did we wisely buy with our three bags of best quality old woollens?' asked Tom, grinning and covering his ears with his hands.

'What else but the loveliest, most miserable dinosaur in all the world,' came the roar.

'And what *isn't* his name?' demanded Clare at the top of her voice.

'Stupid Greenie Greenway,' shouted the children, derisively. They were jigging about and enjoying this enormously.

'So what's his name then?' cried Tom, dramatically pointing to the top of the towering monkey-puzzle tree where towered, even higher, Dear Grumble's small pinched face.

'Dear Grumble, of course,' was the enthusiastic response.

'With a "Price" on the end to avoid confusion,' said Little Billy, quickly. Even though he was still rubbing his sore backside where two rose-thorns were still deeply lodged, he was smiling sympathetically at Dear Grumble Price.

'In fact,' said Tom, generously, 'a Dear Grumble who is going to be taken for walks on his lead, and for games in the park by everyone who remained loyal to me and Clare. So what do you think about that?'

The children cheered for the last time. Not all of the children could go straight home. Some had to return to the empty park to pick up their abandoned and yelping dogs. Little Billy didn't have this chore. His mongrel Socrates had wide intelligent eyes and Little Billy had taught him to untie simple knots with his teeth. He would be waiting at home with a pile of painted ping-pong balls at his paws, for his young master was teaching him how to count.

Tom and Clare stood in their ruined garden and gazed up at the pet they had fought so hard to buy and keep. The cost had been high in many ways, but they agreed it had all been worthwhile. Now they could look forward to the long hot summer days when they would get to know Dear Grumble properly. Days in which to fathom out what ailed him and made him so miserable. They hoped for that special day when they could coax the first wide smile from that sad and gloomy face. Suddenly, without warning,

Dear Grumble's troubled head struck and neatly bit the top off Mr Price's monkey-puzzle tree. The children froze. They froze even more when their mother's raised voice shattered their silent horror.

'Tom, Clare, supper's ready and our favourite quiz show is just starting,' she called through her lace-curtained window. She just happened to be polishing her red-tinted spectacles at the time so luckily she didn't notice that the top of Mr Price's tree had vanished into Dear Grumble's stomach. Again she called, annoyed now. 'For heaven's sake stop fussing over that dinosaur. You'll have plenty of time to play with him in the morning.'

A short time later, supper-trays balanced on their knees, Tom and Clare were relieved to learn that their father had gone to bed early. Nervously they picked at their curried chicken and rice and pretended to watch the quiz show. But all the time they were sneaking glances out of the window to see whether yet more of their father's tree had disappeared. They felt grateful when Mrs Price got up and drew her thick curtains. Then it was time for bed.

Leaving their mother downstairs watching the horror movie, Tom and Clare raced upstairs to look out of the landing window. Their worst fears were confirmed. But for a moment they forgot their worries as they looked down on a

beautiful sight. Dear Grumble was slumped in the very position the children had suggested. The tip of his enormous tail lay outside Mrs Lovejoy's gate, the rest of it snaking along the pavement and smartly turning in through the gap where the Prices fence had once stood. Somehow he'd managed to ease his truck-sized body into some kind of comfort on the lawn, and had trickily corkscrewed around the trunk of the monkey-puzzle tree. Then his long slim neck took over where his bulk left off to snake down the path to the empty garage into which he had poked his miserable head. But it was the trunk of the monkey-puzzle tree that Tom and Clare were now staring at wide-eyed. For that's what it was. Just a trunk or a stump with nothing on the top.

'That's just about it, then, Clare,' breathed Tom, his heart sinking into the soles of his slippers. 'Dear Grumble has blotted his copybook on his very first night by doing the unthinkable.'

'But the tree was dying, wasn't it?' whispered Clare, gnawing on the collar of her nightdress, her frightened eyes huge and white in the dim light on the landing. 'You know how Dad was always having to cut off the withered bits. His monkey-puzzle tree would have stripped itself bare without help eventually . . . wouldn't it?'

Tom nervously shook his head. 'We have to face the facts. Dear Grumble has eaten Dad's living, breathing monkey-puzzle tree. The point is, how much more aggro can he take? What can we do?'

'Well, I'm going to bed,' said Clare, shivering. 'And I'm going to lock my door. If Dad wants a word with us in the morning, will you speak to him, Tom?'

'You're not leaving me to face the music alone,' her brother hissed. 'The lock on my own door is broken but I'll wedge a chair under the handle. If Dad comes raging up the stairs in the morning he can bawl out my DO NOT DIS-TURB GENIUS AT WORK sign.'

'I won't say goodnight, then', replied Clare, savagely. Turning abruptly she padded along the landing to her room. Once inside she clicked the lock, jumped into bed, pulled the duvet over her head and tried to sleep. She didn't, much.

Neither did Tom. Pacing the floor of his own room he tried to think of a way to placate his father. But clear thinking was difficult. In the big double bedroom Mr Price was propped up in bed watching the horror movie. Tom's brain spun as the gurgles and screams and terrible death-threats drifted under his door. Dreading the morning even more he snatched up his wicker-basket bedside chair and wedged it under the door handle. Then he too tried to sleep. But it was difficult.

Midnight passed. Few sounds disturbed the

79

peace of Tom and Clare's village. Dear Grumble's restless stirrings and sleepily muttered 'dear, oh dears' were amongst the few sounds that rent the night. Also, heard by the foxes and the hoot-owls, came the tap-tap-tap of the end of his tail against Mrs Lovejoy's gate. And also his rumbling snores echoing around the cramped confines of Mr Prices car-less garage.

Who was Soon Loved by All

'Are you sure it's gone, dear?' called Mrs Price from her kitchen. She was trying to frizzle bacon and eggs and watch breakfast television at the same time. Now and then she wiped the steam from her red-tinted spectacles and ordered a whining Patch to get back in his basket and from under her feet.

'Of course I'm sure it's gone,' yelled Mr Price from the living room. 'If I say it's gone it's got to be . . . well, most of it . . . come and see for yourself, woman.'

'Don't you use that tone with me, I'm not your "woman",' bristled Mrs Price. She slip-slopped in her red slippers to join him in the shaft of fierce sunlight that was streaming in through the front window. Then she gave a little shriek.

'Oh, my goodness, not Dear Grumble. The children will be heart-broken.'

'Never mind that lump of a dinosaur, what about my monkey-puzzle tree?' shouted her angry husband. 'A stump, that's all he's left me. That ugly great brute has scoffed my tree in the dead of night. Just as well he's scarpered. If he'd had the cheek to hang around he'd be feeling the toe of my boot up his backside right now.'

'Dear, oh dear, oh dear,' consoled Mrs Price. 'Never mind, dear, you can always grow another one. It's the children I'm worried about, though. They thought the world of that new pet of theirs. By the way, dear, have you noticed how much lighter it is in here now that the monkey-puzzle tree is gone?'

The oaths of Mr Price drifted up the stairs and woke the children. Unbarring their doors, Tom and Clare tip-toed out on to the landing. Leaning over the bannister-rail they listened with bated breath to the loud shouts of their father. But it was the words of their mother that caused them to overcome their fear when she said, 'Of course I will miss the monkey-puzzle tree, dear, but what can we say to the children when they find that Dear Grumble is missing?' Tom and Clare raced down the stairs, Clare in tears, Tom shaking with anger.

'Has Dear Grumble run away, Mum?' cried Clare, bursting into the living room in floods of tears.

'He's been stolen more like,' said a grim-faced Tom, entering hard on her heels. 'And we all know by who.'

'Never mind about that prehistoric stomach on legs,' their father bawled. 'I was looking forward to pruning that tree today. I've a good mind to jump in my car and track down that greedy great vandal. He can't have got far on those whacking great clumsy feet. And he's also having to flee on a belly-full of my monkey-puzzle tree. That should slow him down. I only hope he's suffering from severe indigestion – thieves never prosper.'

'Don't be silly dear, you haven't got a car, remember?' chided Mrs Price. 'Anyway, Dear Grumble wouldn't think eating your tree was criminal. Dinosaurs don't think like that. He probably just felt a little peckish in the night. So really he has no earthly reason to run away from home.'

'Exactly,' shouted Tom. 'I say he's been stolen and we know who's done it! I'm going outside to look for clues.'

'And I'm coming with you,' cried Clare, chasing after him as he raced for the front door.

'Not a word from those two about my tree, you'll notice,' yelled Mr Price. 'Just glance at my garden out there. It's like looking at a scene from that film we watched last Tuesday. What

was it now . . . *All Quiet on the Western Front*?
I'm telling you, woman, a bomb would have
caused less damage than that great green lump
has done.'

'I've told you, don't call me "woman",' said
Mrs Price, sharply. Then reprovingly, 'And it
was Wednesday, dear. That film was shown last
Wednesday. Remember they screened it after
that new quiz show. The one where you never
got one answer right.'

'Well, I've got one answer right this morning,'
snapped Mr Price. 'That dinosaur ate my
monkey-puzzle tree in the night and was so filled
with guilt that he took it on the lam. Patch once
went missing for days when he pinched a pork
chop from my plate and afterwards tucked into
my After Eight mints. What's the betting that
dinosaur is heading for Offa's Dyke and the
Welsh border . . .?'

'Wrong, Dad,' shouted Tom, rushing back
into the room. 'Dear Grumble may have eaten
your tree but he's certainly not trying to find
refuge in Wales. Show them the note, Clare. It
must be a forgery.'

'Dear Grumble left a note?' said Mrs Price,
surprised. 'Now that is clever, Patch didn't
when he pinched your father's pork chop and
mints. And stop howling, Patch, it's much
too early in the morning. Get back in your
basket. You were saying, dear about Dear

84

Grumble leaving a note . . .'

'No, he didn't, but the thief did,' cried Clare, brandishing a slip of paper. 'Just listen to this. TO THE PRICES. I HAVE RUN AWAY TO MY PROPER HOME WHERE I WILL BE BETTER TREATED THAN I AM AT YOURS. DO NOT TRY TO FIND ME. SIGNED, GREENIE GREENWAY.'

'But the thief made a terrible mistake,' shouted Tom, his face livid with rage. He snatched the note from Clare and pointed to some printed words in the right-hand corner. 'Read that, Dad.'

'GREENWAYS SUPER SHOPPING STORE,' read Mr Price aloud. Then his face clouded. Then it turned bright pink. At the same time he bit so hard on the stem of his pipe that it snapped clean off. 'Those Greenways again,' he roared. 'Not content with robbing folk blind in their shops, and selling honest people duff cars while they ride about in Rolls Royces, they have to steal pets from little children.'

'You've changed your tune, dear,' said Mrs Price, mildly. 'But surely you can't accuse Mr Greenway? Not even he would be so childish.'

'It's that Felicity,' said Tom, his face like stone. 'When she sets her mind to something she never rests until she gets it.'

'Like trying to persuade you to go to Green-way Towers for tea,' agreed Clare, nodding

85

furiously. 'So what are we going to do? About Dear Grumble, I mean?'

'You march up there and take him back of course,' exploded Mr Price, his monkey-puzzle tree quite forgotten. 'And if that cheeky little madam won't give him up, tell her that I'll be round there with a policeman to see her father. I'd planned to anyway. I think the law will be very interested in my car. So, off you go, you

86

two, and don't come back without that dino-saur.'

'And you can take Patch with you,' said Mrs Price, dragging the reluctant dog from his basket and snapping on his hated lead. 'He'll enjoy the walk.'

Patch was certain he wouldn't enjoy the walk up to Greenway Towers. For the thought of coming back with the dreaded dinosaur appalled him. But he was given little choice. Throughout the journey he hung back on his lead, whining piteously. The Price trio were soon joined by some of the village children. For a while the quiet village lanes were filled with the muffled drum-ming of trainers on flagstones, and the low buzz of angry voices.

Soon the jagged-glass walls of Greenway Towers loomed into view. Crowding around the huge iron gates the children peered through and up the long gravelled drive. To the left of the large ivy-covered house was a small copse of oaks and poplars and holly-bushes.

Though his body was hidden from view the miserable head of Dear Grumble could be plainly seen above the tall trees. He seemed to be eating himself silly, even though his 'dear, oh dear, oh dears' rang out. There was little wind that day but the tops of the trees were being thrashed about as if in a hurricane.

'Come out and show yourself, Greenway,'

shouted Tom though the bars of the gates. 'We know you're in there and we can see Dear Grumble above your trees. Me and Clare have come for what's ours, so hand him over.'

The sleek and freshly-scrubbed figure of Felicity suddenly appeared in the doorway of the mansion-house. She looked very pretty, Tom thought, much against his will. Bouncing up the drive in a new set of trainers, Felicity was as cocky and as brave as ever, undaunted by the crowd of hostile and jeering children.

'What do you lot want?' she asked, defiantly. 'And don't you kick our gates like that. My dad has to pay Jill and Tim's dad to paint it. He does a lot of odd jobs for us, being out of work all the time.'

Jill and Tim blushed deeply. They gained a little comfort from the words of Little Billy. For the clever, likeable lad hated show-off Felicity who thought that money was a substitute for brains. He remarked that such cheap paint could only have come from the Greenway Do-it-Yourself Shop, but Felicity dismissed him with a toss of her blonde pony-tail.

'You know very well what we want,' snapped Clare, her fists white as she grasped the bars of the gate. 'We have come to take Dear Grumble home. And don't say he isn't here, for we can see his sad head above the trees.'

'No you can't,' retorted Felicity. 'The only

head poking above our trees belongs to my pet dinosaur, Greenie Greenway.'

The huge gates almost shook as the children on them gasped. They had all heard some lies in their lives but that one was such a whopper, such a downright cheek that many of them were quite speechless. But not Billy:

'Felicity Greenway,' he began, whipping out his notebook and a red biro from his blazer-pocket. 'Felicity, are you trying to say that the dinosaur head poking above your dad's trees is a different one from the Special Offer the Prices bought from the rag-and-bone man? Because if you are I must warn you that as far as this village knows, there is only one dinosaur still roaming the world, namely Dear Grumble, the rest being extinct. And even if there was another one knocking about it would be too much of a coincidence that he should turn up in our quiet little village, wearing the same miserable expression as Dear Grumble Price. I am bound to caution you that I am taking notes, so let's have the truth, please.'

'Oh, shut up, Little Billy,' snapped Tom. 'You know as well as I do that dinosaur is Dear Grumble.'

'So what are we waiting for?' bellowed a boy at the back of the crush round the gates.

'Let's storm Greenway Towers and rescue Dear Grumble before he grows to love this beautiful big garden more than he liked the Prices' poky place.'

'Set one foot inside our gates and I'll phone my dad and he'll come racing home in his big Rolls Royce with the spanner in the glove compartment,' warned Felicity, her wiry hands grasping the bars of the gates as she prepared to hold them shut against all comers.

'You send for your dad and we'll send Patch to fetch ours, and he'll come racing here in his car,' countered Tom, furiously. 'But we don't need our dad to fight our battles, Greenway. Get away from this gate, we're coming in.'

Gripping the bars of the gate he began to push with all his might. From her side Felicity did the same. The other children stood back. They sensed that this was a private battle. Eye to eye through the bars, their trainers gripping then slipping, Tom and Felicity waged their private war. And surprisingly, Felicity seemed to be winning it. Clare, noticing Tom's humiliation, flung herself at the bars to help him. So did Jill and Tim for personal reasons they were too embarrassed to talk about. Against such odds the wiry Felicity was flung to the ground as the gates flew open. At once Tom and Clare and the rest of the children were in and running for the copse to reclaim Dear Grumble.

'Hey, what are you little ruffians doing in my garden?' shouted a man from the drive. It was

91

Mr Greenway who had just squealed up in his Rolls Royce. He stood on the path, one fist shaking angrily, the other clutching a big bag of money. Felicity stood sobbing into his waistcoat.

Mr Greenway yelled again. 'What have you done to my little Flick? I'll have the law on you.'

Frightened, but determined they would never be parted from their pet again, Tom and Clare emerged from the trees clutching Dear Grumble's tatty piece of string. Obediently, and uninterested in the commotion he had caused, Dear Grumble shambled behind them flanked by a protective cordon of children. His 'dear, oh dears' were muffled, for his mouth was stuffed with an oak branch.

'We are taking Dear Grumble back where he

belongs' Mr Greenway, said Tom, defiantly. 'And because right is on our side we are doing it in broad daylight. We don't creep about in the dead of night stealing people's pets, leaving forged notes.'

'Are you accusing my little Flick of stealing her own pet dinosaur?' roared Mr Greenway. 'Right, I've had quite enough of you Prices. Hand that lead over to my little girl and get out of my garden and stay out.'

'Never,' said Tom, stubbornly. Irritably he shrugged off Felicity, who had run across and was tugging at his T-shirt as usual, her pretty blue eyes looking pleadingly up at him. Meanwhile Clare was beseeching:

'Patch, run and fetch your master. Fetch, Patch. After Eight mints, boy. Fetch.' But Patch was having none of it. He had no intention of being forced to be number two pet in the Price household. So Clare, in desperation, raced off to fetch her father herself. In the meantime an irate Mr Greenway was contacting the police station on his car phone.

But Mr Price, despite his painful bunions, beat him to it. If the constable hadn't stopped to finish his cup of tea and his Kit-Kat, he would have been in time to prevent the fight.

'Tom,' snapped Mr Price. 'Give me Dear Grumble's lead. Now, Greenway, I'm going to walk out of those gates with this dinosaur. Try

and stop me and you'll be one very sorry shop-
keeper.'

Just as he began to limp out of the gates with
Dear Grumble in tow, Mr Greenway rushed up
behind him roaring with rage and hit him over
the head with his heavy bag of money.

'Dear, oh dear, oh dear,' mourned Dear
Grumble, chomping away on his oak branch. He
shuffled his huge feet nervously as the two men
fought and grappled underneath him.

'This is for the duff car you sold me,' cried Mr Price, lunging to black Mr Greenway's eye. 'Now you have a real reason to strut around in dark glasses.'

'Always been jealous of me, haven't you, Price?' shouted Mr Greenway as he stamped on his rival's bunions. 'Ever since we were kids you've envied me. Just because I was the village go-getter and worked hard to get on in the world. And what have you got? A miserable little semi and a nine-to-five job in somebody else's office, and a ridiculous monkey-puzzle tree you're always fussing and clipping at. Was growing that the extent of your ambition, Price?'

'And Mr Price hasn't even got a monkey-puzzle tree, now,' said Little Billy who had been watching the fight with interest. 'But then he wouldn't have had it much longer anyway, it was dying.'

'You keep out of this, clever-clogs,' said Mr Price, stepping back and straightening his tie, his head held proudly high. He addressed the puffing Mr Greenway. 'Mrs Price and I may not have much money, but what we do have is worth much more. A couple of happy and good-natured kids, for instance. Not a spoiled brat like your daughter. And now we have Dear Grumble, who is welcome to share our home with us.'

Patch whined and pawed at his master's torn trousers.

'As number two pet, of course,' said Mr Price, patting his faithful friend. 'For though Patch stinks to high heaven most of the time, we love him. We will love Dear Grumble too, despite his miserable face, and the way he ignores folk as if they weren't there. So, Greenway, get out of my way, for come hell or high water I'm taking this dinosaur home . . .'

But was Ordered Away

'Oh no you're not,' said a firm voice. The village constable stepped out of his little car with the light on top and took hold of Dear Grumble's lead. 'I am taking this dinosaur into custody. If his presence in our quiet village is going to cause feuds and brawls then it's my duty to put a stop to it. You, young Tom, I hear you bought this dinosaur from that rascally rag-and-bone man?'

'Yes, sir,' replied Tom, quietly. 'But we paid a fair price for him.'

'I'm sure you did, lad,' the constable said, patting his head kindly. 'But we can't have him causing all this trouble. That's why I'm forced to arrest him and lock him up in my car-park at the back of my police station until such time as the rag-and-bone man calls again.'

'And what will happen when he calls again, Constable Hobbleday?' asked Clare, faintly.

'Then you and Tom will return him and swap him for something – for something more peaceful,' was the stern reply. 'Like a balloon on a stick, for instance, or a goldfish, two, even.'

'No, no, please don't arrest Dear Grumble,' begged Clare, sobbing. 'He will waste away in jail, I just know he will.'

'Please don't make us take him back to the rag-and-bone man,' implored Tom. 'Dear Grumble will only be dragged off to the next village and sold to someone who won't understand him.'

'Which means he'll no longer be a Price,' said Little Billy, gravely. 'Dear Grumble will suffer a terrible identity crisis if Constable Hobbleday carries out his duty.'

'Just be careful I don't arrest you, Little Billy know-it-all,' said the constable, tapping the pocket where he kept his rarely-used truncheon. He turned back to Tom and Clare and Felicity, who was stamping her new trainers bad-temperedly. 'There is a way out, of course. If the three of you agree to own him between you then the dinosaur can stay. So what do you say?'

'Never, Greenie Greenway belongs to me alone,' screamed Felicity, and kicked the constable's shin. 'If he's to live anywhere he'll live in my garden.'

'For that, young madam, you can come and

sweep my car-park every day next week,' snapped the constable, wincing with pain. He turned to Tom and Clare. 'And what do you two say?'

'I say that Dear Grumble should live where his heart is,' said Tom, stoutly. 'That is curled round my dad's monkey-puzzle tree stump.'

'And you two, who ought to be ashamed of yourselves, brawling in front of children like

that,' said the policeman, sternly eyeing the sheepish grown-ups.

'Why should my little Flick have to share her pet with a pair of ruffians?' blustered Mr Greenway.

'And why should my kids be forced to kowtow to the whims of that spoiled brat?' snapped Mr Price, glaring at his enemy. 'I'm sorry, Constable, but I'm digging my heels in over this one.'

'Then I'm left with no choice,' said the constable, as he tied Dear Grumble's lead to the back bumper of his little car. He glanced across at the crestfallen Price children. 'He comes this way each Friday, doesn't he? I mean the rag-and-bone man? Right, next Friday come and pick up this dinosaur from my car-park. You will then take him back and swap him for something more sensible. Oh, and make sure you come every day to the police station to feed him as I don't suppose he'll find the prison diet very filling. What does he eat, by the way?'

'Blackberry bushes, holly-boughs, oak trees and the odd poplar-top,' replied Tom, gloomily.

'And monkey-puzzle trees when his nerves are bad,' said Little Billy, knowingly. 'And I think I know why his nerves are bad. I've worked it our scientifically. I reckon that Dear Grumble is pining for someone. Probably someone close he hasn't seen for a long time. Probably somebody

101

like his grandfather. Which brings me to a point of law, Constable Hobbleday. I have been taking notes and according to the evidence Dear Grumble hasn't committed a criminal offence that I can see. Do you realise that Dear Grumble could have you up for false arrest?'

'Just watch it, you cheeky little devil,' warned the constable, tapping the pocket where he kept his handcuffs. He then addressed everyone. 'Okay, I am ordering you to disperse at once. Unless either of you gentlemen want me to jot down some assault charges?'

Mr Greenway, who was nursing his eye, and Mr Price, who was favouring his throbbing toes, shook their heads.

'I thought not,' said the constable with a grin. He drove slowly away. Slowly because he was a kind policeman and didn't want Dear Grumble to trip over his large clumsy feet and fall flat on his miserable face. The children followed glumly all the way to the police station. As the procession approached the High Street a large crowd of shoppers gathered. By now everyone in the village knew about Dear Grumble, or Greenie Greenway as Felicity encouraged her few friends to call him. Only Patch wore a smile as Dear Grumble was finally locked up in the car park at the back of the police station. He was so happy that he joyfully chased his tail on the pavement outside. But then he would, wouldn't he?

Every day Tom and Clare and the children visited Dear Grumble in his lonely prison to feed him his favourite branches and boughs and stuff. Tom and Clare tried to keep his chin up by telling him that perhaps the rag-and-bone man had wobbled a wheel off his cart, and would not come. Felicity also called every day. But then she had to, to sweep out the car-park. But she didn't mind at all. While whisking round the courtyard with her broom she was planning a cunning SAS-type escape. Thursday, the day before Greenie Greenway had to go back to the rag-and-bone man, would be D-DAY.

'Just hang on, Greenie,' she whispered to him as she swept up around his toes. 'I'll get you out of here, you'll see. And then we'll run away together. We'll go where no one will ever find us. Except Tom, of course. We'll send him a post card. Just grit your teeth and hang in there, Greenie.'

'Dear, oh dear, oh dear,' moaned the dinosaur, his huge neck snaking over the wall and down the High Street where his head was patted a lot by sympathetic shoppers – not that their affection made any difference.

Thursday morning came. Constable Hobbleday was sitting in his office with his large boots propped up on his desk, drinking his tea and eating his Kit-Kat when he heard the sound of his double gates being trundled open. Strolling out-

side to the car-park he was just in time to see the
dinosaur bolting through the gates led by Felicity
all dressed in black, and wearing a frightening-
looking gas-mask.

'Hey, bring back my prisoner,' shouted the
constable. He dashed after them and drawing his
truncheon, rapped the dinosaur smartly on one
of his enormous toes. It was a bad mistake.
Snaking down his long neck the dinosaur picked
up the policeman, swept him high into the air,

and plopped him neatly on the police station roof. Then the huge green pet and Felicity belted down the High Street.

'Out of the way, I'm armed and desperate,' cried Felicity to the screaming shoppers as she raced down the road, the green giant sending the milkman's float crashing on its side as they dashed past.

'Call the fire brigade,' yelled Constable Hobbleday from his high perch. 'And don't anyone try to apprehend that dinosaur, he's highly dangerous. The law will deal with him as soon as I get down.'

It seemed that Felicity was heading for the railway station. How she expected to get a dinosaur in a railway carriage was a mystery. She was screaming at the ticket-lady for two-one way tickets to anywhere when the fire engine, with Constable Hobbleday clinging to the ladder, caught up with her. Protesting and

kicking, she was unmasked.

'So it's you, eh?' stormed Constable Hobbleday. 'I should have known it. Right, back to the police station both of you. We'd better call your father, young lady – you've a lot of explaining to do.'

Wrapping the dinosaur's lead round one wrist, and gripping the collar of Felicity's black ski-suit with his other hand, he began to march them back to the police station. Meanwhile the village children had arrived in the High Street.

'Felicity tried to spring Dear Grumble,' said Little Billy to Tom and Clare who had just come panting up. 'Her mistake was making for the railway station. How could she possibly believe she could have got away with it? But it was a nice try. I expect she will be charged and sent to one of those special schools for a short, sharp shock.'

The children lined the road as Constable Hobbleday, Felicity and Dear Grumble passed by. The constable was rubbing the seat of his pants where Dear Grumble's teeth had dug in. Felicity, blonde hair flying in the wind, looked defiant and as pretty as ever, thought Tom. As for Dear Grumble, he was muttering, 'Dear, oh dear, oh dear,' as he ambled back into custody. On the understanding that Mr Greenway would give Felicity a good spanking, she was allowed to go free. But everyone knew that Mr Greenway wouldn't lay a finger on his beloved Flick. As for

Dear Grumble, how does one punish a dinosaur who couldn't be made any more miserable than he already was? And then it was Friday . . .

Then Came Home Double-Special

Tom and Clare sat gloomily on their front gate, Dear Grumble hulking beside them. Once again they were waiting for the rag-and-bone man to call, but this time they were dreading his visit.

Inside their house the goldfish bowl was ready once more. Mrs Price had run her duster round it and Mr Price had filled it full of fresh water before he went to work on the bus. It now sat on the dining-room table looking pretty indeed with its sandy bottom, its concrete snail and the plastic frond of weed. Their father had promised to bring home a little plastic cave for the goldfish to swim in and out of, or two goldfish, even. He said it was no bother for he had to stop off to pick up a monkey-puzzle sapling anyway. He had tried to cheer Tom and Clare up that Friday morning. But it was hard going. How could a goldfish, two, even, possibly take the place of Dear Grumble, in spite of all his moods? But alas, Constable Hobbleday had laid down the law and Tom and Clare could only obey.

The village children had turned out in force to say goodbye. Slumped on the pavement outside the Prices' house their conversation was muted and moody. Even Little Billy had none of his 'theories' to lecture them with, he was so upset. Because this was to be a sad goodbye he had respectfully taken off his school cap and stuffed it in his pocket, revealing a rare glimpse of his flaming red hair. Felicity was there of course. She was subdued too. All the children had cold-

shouldered her. She tried to clamber up on the
gate beside Tom, even though he did push her
down again. So she settled for hanging on to the
sleeve of his T-shirt. And then suddenly they all
heard it. The ominous sound of hooves clip-
clopping up the lane.

It was a sad procession that wound down the
lane to meet the rag-and-bone man. At the front
were Tom and Clare, their trainers scuffing, their
heads downcast. Between them ambled the
mighty bulk of Dear Grumble, moaning as
usual, his jaws snapping at the poplar-tops he'd
missed on the way up. Ranged beside and behind
were the village children, Little Billy busily
jotting down notes about anything that caught

his scientific eye. Felicity had managed to worm her way to Tom's side again. Even when he shoved her into the ditch from time to time she hung on to his T-shirt sleeve. And then, there in the bend in the lane, they saw it. At that moment an extraordinary change came over Dear Grumble. His pinched face suddenly lit up and he grinned from ear to ear. Eyes sparkling, huge feet dancing a little dinosaur jig, he lunged towards the back of the old man's cart spilling Tom and Clare to the ground as they tried to hang on to his lead. In seconds his grin was united with another, though lower, grin as two dinosaurs said 'hello' as only two joyous dinosaurs can. In the meantime the old man was smiling down at the children, his false teeth as crooked as ever. He knew quite well what they were goggling at, but being a bit of a tease he didn't let on that he'd noticed.

'And what can I do for you lovely little ladies and gentlemen?' he grinned. 'As you see I've got plenty of wares, so where are your old woollens? Or are you just taking your Special Offer for a brisk walk?'

'Just tell me how many best quality old woollens you want,' shrieked Felicity, her cornflower blue eyes nearly bulging from her head as she gazed at the prize she meant to have. 'And if anyone else bids higher, I will go twice as high and then twice again.'

'Ah, the scruffy little girl with the rich daddy,' said the old man, recognising her. He rubbed his horny hands. 'So, I expect you'll be wanting to hear my selling-spiel? Well, here goes . . . for one bag of old woollens you can have a balloon on a stick . . .'

'On your bike,' yelled Felicity, ignoring the

boy who had crept up behind to pull the pink ribbon from her pony-tail.

'Very well,' said the old man, pretending to be hurt. 'How about a goldfish for two bags of old woollens, two, even . . . ?

'Go and take a running jump,' bawled Felicity, wincing with pain as somebody stepped on her 'centre-court' trainers.

'Spoilt little brat, aren't you?' said the man, mildly. 'But never mind, if there's nothing I can interest you in I can always move on to the next village.'

'You move one inch and I'll run and get my dad,' threatened Felicity.

'I take your point,' said the rag-and-bone man, hurriedly. 'So what is it you want?'

'You can tell me point blank what you want for the object tied to the back of your cart,' snapped Felicity, her nervous fingers toying with a thread she'd unravelled from Tom's T-shirt.

'You'll be referring to my Special Offer, no doubt?' said the old man, grinning again. 'The one acting all lovey-dovey with the one I sold to the solemn lad and his tear-stained sister over there.'

'That's the one,' nodded Felicity emphatically. 'Just name your price and hang on for five minutes and then you won't get your head bashed in with my dad's spanner.'

'Ah, now,' sighed the old man, shaking his

114

head. 'We are talking about a Special, Special Offer now. As you can see, The Nipper is a dinosaur of such quality as to take the breath away. Note his glittering emerald skin and scales, the proud sweep of his tail, his clear eyes. Notice how light he is on his feet, and imagine him playing sweeper in your next village football match . . .'

'I'll take him,' cried Felicity, cutting the spiel short. 'And I'll fight anyone who tries to step in between me and my new Greenie Greenway.'

'Okay,' shrugged the rag-and-bone man. Then his eyes narrowed greedily. 'But The Nipper will cost you four bags of best quality old woollens.'

'You've got em', rapped Felicity. And off she hared up the lane. Arriving back at Greenway Towers she cruelly tipped her screaming little brother from his newly-mended little red car and once again piled her bags aboard. Having only three bags with one to go, and having so little time to gather them together, she dashed into the hall and snatched her mother's new mink coat from its peg. Minutes later she was back in the bend in the lane, her breath coming in huge gasps as she leaned against the old horse's backside to recover. Despite their earlier feelings the children just had to cheer her. Tom thought how attractive she looked when not dolled up in ribbons and flounces – like for the village Miss Junior Beauty

Queen contests, for instance, which she always won, or for Sunday School prize-givings, which she never did. Tom liked her as she looked now, a bit scruffy and tousled, and with her blue eyes flashing – not that he would ever admit to it.

'Now that is a marvellous bit of stuff,' the old man said, fingering through one of the bags. Suddenly he choked as he spied the mink coat. He tried to look casual, but was desperate to get away. He jerked his thumb over his shoulder.

'You, little lady, are now the proud owner of The Nipper there. Untie and enjoy. And may you have lots of happy games of netball together.'

Amid cheers Felicity ran to the back of the cart and untied 'The Nipper' from the back of the cart ready to lead him away. But the shiny green dinosaur refused to go. He wouldn't leave Dear Grumble's side. The pair of them looked very miserable indeed. 'Dear, oh dear, oh dear,' they moaned in unison.

'So what are you kids waiting for?' said the old man, looking puzzled as he hoisted Felicity's woollens aboard his cart. 'The deal's complete so take your pets to the park or wherever, for I've got balloooms and goldfish to swap in the next village.'

'You've also got another Special Offer to get rid of,' said Tom, trying to swallow the lump in his throat as he gazed up at gloomy Dear Grumble. 'You see, Rag-and-bone man, the constable has ordered me and Clare to swap Dear Grumble for something that will cause less friction. So we have decided to settle for what we should have had in the first place. We were thinking of a goldfish, two, even.'

'Not that we want to lose Dear Grumble,' wept Clare. 'It's just that Felicity Greenway kept claiming that he belonged to her, which led to a fight and the banning of Dear Grumble from our

117

village. And it just isn't fair. Felicity caused all that trouble and now she owns The Nipper, while we own nothing.'

'Oh, yes you do,' said the old man who was deep down very kind. 'You owned your Dear Grumble from the moment we did our swap. For we in the rag-trade have a firm policy. And that policy is never to swap goldfish for dinosaurs, especially used ones. And I can see that Dear Grumble has been run ragged by the state of his feet. No, I'm sorry, but I can't take that dinosaur back under any circumstances.'

'Does that mean we are lumbered with him?'; gasped Tom, his eyes shining. 'Does it mean that the constable will have to like Dear Grumble or lump him?'

'Well, I wouldn't want to tangle with the law,' said the old man, hastily.

'In other words you are saying, "Be off with you and your dinosaur, you'll get no swapped goldfish from me"?' cried Clare. 'Would you even go so far as to order your nice old horse to bite us on our way?'

'I would,' said the old man with a twinkle, 'Though old Dozy much prefers oats.'

'It's quite extraordinary,' said Little Billy, scratching his nose with his green biro. 'But I've been comparing Dear Grumble and The Nipper. And though Dear Grumble is larger, and a less brilliant shade of green, and though he is a mite heavier on his feet when he dances, and though he doesn't flash the same toothpaste smile, all in all the two of them could easily be big brother and little brother. Could you explain this, Mr rag-and-bone man? And do you mind if I take your answers down in the form of notes?'

'Not at all,' smiled the old man. 'My, but you are a clever chap. In fact you are quite right. Those two dinosaurs, with their necks twined together at the back of my cart, are indeed brothers. Unfortunately they were parted in the Cash and Carry warehouse where I get all my dinosaurs. But it's nice to see them reunited, eh? Don't they make a cracking sight, the pair of em?'

'They certainly do,' shouted Tom, delightedly. 'No wonder Dear Grumble was always muttering, 'Dear, oh dear, oh dear.' Who wouldn't if they were suddenly parted from their much-loved little brother?'

'Well, they'll never be parted again,' vowed Clare, vehemently. She looked anxiously up at the rag-and-bone man, who was flicking his reins and clicking to his tired old horse to move on. 'Are you quite sure that your policy forbids you to take used goods back? Even if a constable came speeding after you in a little car and demanded that you did?'

'I know my rights under the law,' replied the old man as he rolled away on his squealing cart.

'A sale is a sale, and all the constables in the world won't tell me different. Goodbye, then. See you all next week. Oh, and I'm expecting in a batch of pterosaurs if you're interested . . .'

'Put me down for the one with the widest wing-span,' shouted Little Billy. 'And if I were you I'd get that rear off-side wheel seen to. It's ready to wobble off according to my scientific calculations.'

But it didn't. And it probably never would. For rag-and-bone carts, and the horses that pulled them, and the old men who rode them, always looked ready to fall apart, to vanish into the dust of an age long gone, that was the beauty of them.

Now the jubilant party of children were ready to leave the bend in the lane. But before they did, Tom thought it was about time they made their peace with Felicity. After all, if everyone agreed that the dinosaur brothers were to live a long and peaceful life together, being constantly at war with each other might drive their two pets back to their 'dear, oh dear, oh dearing' which would make everyone miserable all over again.

'I've been thinking, Felicity,' he said 'I suppose you will be taking The Nipper back to Greenway Towers.'

'I'll be taking Greenie Greenway the second back to Greenway Towers,' corrected the girl,

120

gazing adoringly up at her pet.

'But for the sake of the happiness of them both, wouldn't it be kinder if we allowed them to live together?' said Tom.

'Okay,' replied Felicity, happily. 'They can

both come and live at Greenway Towers. And you can come and see them whenever you like.'

'What are you saying, Tom?' said Clare, aghast. 'After all we've gone through!'

'I think that would be very upsetting for Clare,' said Tim, blushing beet-red. 'I think you should have more consideration for her, Tom.'

'I think Tom's being far too generous to Felicity,' said Jill, angrily. 'There are folk more worthy of his generosity than her.'

At that moment the rag-and-bone man clicked to his horse and began to squeal away up the lane. 'Why don't you arrange for your Special Offers to live together,' he called. 'That seems the most sensible plan to me. But take no notice of a poor rag-and-bone man, who will never understand the mystery of kids. Goodbye, and I won't forget your Special Offer pterosaur, young Einstein.'

'Thank you very much, Mr Rag-and-bone man,' called Little Billy. 'And in return I'll bring my engineering tool-set and fix that wonky wheel on your cart.'

'Don't bother,' replied the old man, hastily. 'Just get plenty of best quality old woollens together, you're going to need them.' And that was the last they saw of him for another week.

'Now that is a good idea,' said Clare. Why can't the dinosaurs live together? They could fit into our front garden with a squeeze.'

'That isn't what I meant at all,' said Tom, irritably. 'Why can't the dinosaurs live together in the park? Then everyone will have a fair share of walking them and things. So, what do you say, Felicity?'

Felicity looked straight at Tom and to everyone's amazement gave in.

'My Greenie Greenway the second can live in the park with Dear Grumble on one condition,' said Felicity, firmly. 'Tom must promise to come to tea at our house every Sunday.'

'And what if he doesn't want to?' flared Jill.

'Oh, I don't know,' said Tom, trying to sound casual. In fact he quite liked the idea. 'If it means The Nipper and Dear Grumble can enjoy life together, I don't really mind going to Felicity's for tea now and again.'

'So that's that then,' said Clare, happily. 'Shall we go home, for I'm dying to see Mum's face when she sees Dear Grumble back again. She'll cry with happiness, I know she will.'

'But what about Constable Hobbleday?' said Little Billy, being practical again. 'I've got a feeling there will soon be two dinosaurs in his car-park prison.'

'Oh don't be a misery-guts, Little Billy,' scolded Clare. 'I'm sure we can smooth the constable round.'

'Not forgetting that we'll also have to smooth the park-keeper,' Little Billy persisted. 'He's not going to take kindly to a pair of dinosaurs lumbering over his grass, and plunging in his boating-lake when people are out in his boats. I only trod on one of his daisies once and he chased me all the way home.'

'We'll cross the hurdles of Constable Hobbleday and the park-keeper when we come to them,' said Tom. 'In the meantime we'll look on the bright side and march our new pets up the lane so that they can begin their new life together. Come on, gang.'

To the sound of cheers Tom and Clare and Felicity took their dinosaurs by their leads and led them up the lane towards home. Behind them came the rest of the village children, not caring a hoot that their dogs were still tied up in the empty park. Last of all came Little Billy, his legs pumping furiously as he pedalled the little red car up the hill. He was anxious to get home and swot up about pterosaurs. He was wondering whether it was possible to train one to sit on his wrist like a hawk.

In the meantime, Mrs Price would be thawing out the television suppers and watching the television at the same time. Next door, Mrs Lovejoy would be feeding Goldie his ant's-eggs, pleased that the hulking shadow of Dear Grumble no longer blocked out her light. Around and about the village Mr Greenway would be stopping off at his many shops to collect the money in his money-bag, the heavy spanner tucked into the belt of his trousers. As for Mr Price, he would be leaving his stuffy office to stop off on his way home to pick up a monkey-puzzle tree sapling, and the plastic cave for the goldfish to swim in and out of, two goldfish, even. And finally, the constable would be sitting with his feet up drinking his tea and breaking his Kit-Kat, sighing with relief that the wretched dinosaur was no longer about to interfere with the smooth process of the law. He had yet to learn that he was in for a busy day . . . and night.

But for Dear Grumble and The Nipper, that day and night and all the following days and nights would be happy ones if the children had anything to do with it. Their two pets already looked blissful in their togetherness as they shambled up the hill to their new home in the park, their necks entwined as Dear Grumble tenderly shoved poplar-tops, the occasional hawthorn bush, and the odd holly-bough into his little brother's smiling mouth.

Also by W. J. Corbett

THE BEAR WHO STOOD ON HIS HEAD

Ben the bear is as round as a butterball and his eyes are the colour of chewed toffee. He is the baby bear of the family. But wherever he goes, disaster follows! His sister and brother are fed up with him spoiling their adventures and get very angry. But when Ben gets upset, he stands on his head and weeps until tears trickle into this ears . . .

Ben the roly-poly bear is simply irresistible!

A selected list of titles available from Mammoth

While every effort is made to keep prices low, it is sometimes necessary to increase prices at short notice. Mandarin Paperbacks reserves the right to show new retail prices on covers which may differ from those previously advertised in the text or elsewhere.

The prices shown below were correct at the time of going to press.

☐ 7497 0366 0	**Dilly the Dinosaur**	Tony Bradman	£2.50
☐ 7497 0137 4	**Flat Stanley**	Jeff Brown	£2.50
☐ 7497 0306 7	**The Chocolate Touch**	P Skene Catling	£2.50
☐ 7497 0568 X	**Dorrie and the Goblin**	Patricia Coombs	£2.50
☐ 7497 0114 5	**Dear Grumble**	W J Corbett	£2.50
☐ 7497 0054 8	**My Naughty Little Sister**	Dorothy Edwards	£2.50
☐ 7497 0723 2	**The Little Prince (colour ed.)**	A Saint-Exupery	£3.99
☐ 7497 0305 9	**Bill's New Frock**	Anne Fine	£2.99
☐ 7497 0590 6	**Wild Robert**	Diana Wynne Jones	£2.50
☐ 7497 0661 9	**The Six Bullerby Children**	Astrid Lindgren	£2.50
☐ 7497 0319 9	**Dr Monsoon Taggert's Amazing Finishing Academy**	Andrew Matthews	£2.50
☐ 7497 0420 9	**I Don't Want To!**	Bel Mooney	£2.50
☐ 7497 0833 6	**Melanie and the Night Animal**	Gillian Rubinstein	£2.50
☐ 7497 0264 8	**Akimbo and the Elephants**	A McCall Smith	£2.50
☐ 7497 0048 3	**Friends and Brothers**	Dick King-Smith	£2.50
☐ 7497 0795 X	**Owl Who Was Afraid of the Dark**	Jill Tomlinson	£2.99

All these books are available at your bookshop or newsagent, or can be ordered direct from the publisher. Just tick the titles you want and fill in the form below.

Mandarin Paperbacks, Cash Sales Department, PO Box 11, Falmouth, Cornwall TR10 9EN.

Please send cheque or postal order, no currency, for purchase price quoted and allow the following for postage and packing:

UK including BFPO   £1.00 for the first book, 50p for the second and 30p for each additional book ordered to a maximum charge of £3.00.

Overseas including Eire   £2 for the first book, £1.00 for the second and 50p for each additional book thereafter.

NAME (Block letters) ....

ADDRESS ....

....

☐ I enclose my remittance for ....

☐ I wish to pay by Access/Visa Card Number ⬚⬚⬚⬚⬚⬚⬚⬚⬚⬚⬚⬚⬚⬚⬚⬚

Expiry Date ⬚⬚⬚⬚